GIVING
My Heart To A
Gangsta

By Londyn

Dedication

This book is dedicated to anyone still chasing that hood life thinking that fast money and fast cars is living. The hood dream comes with a hefty price. Will you be ready to pay when the streets come to collect?

Chapter One
(Katrina)

"How many times do I have to tell your fast ass to come straight home from school, Katrina?" My mother barked as soon as I walked through the door.

"I have no control of how fast the bus run. I'm a passenger, not the driver," I mumbled under my breath, attempting to walk away.

"Katrina, don't get the shit slapped out of you for thinking that your ass is grown. Now get in there and clean those dishes, then do your damn homework since you want to be smart lipped today!" She shouted, causing me to roll my eyes.

She was home all day so I'm not understanding as to why I'm the one held responsible to come home and wash dishes that she made. I stormed down the hallway to my bedroom pissed off and sick of her mistaking me for the fucking maid up in this bitch. Her lazy fucking boyfriend is the one that demands breakfast every morning, which she accommodates. Not caring enough to fix me anything but wants me to wash their dishes. I was so sick of her and her boyfriend. I couldn't wait to leave up out of here because I was tired of being treated like a damn child.

"Katrina, how long does it take for you to change your clothes? You have five minutes to get your ass out here and do what the hell I told you to do!" She shouted from the hallway, causing me to suck my teeth.

I left my room and walked to the kitchen to wash the dishes because she wasn't going to leave me alone until they were done. I was slamming shit around because of all the dishes in the sink, which was ridiculous, but all I did was add to her frustration.

"Slam another one of my fucking dishes, Katrina. I dare you," she challenged, now standing in front of me with a belt in her hand.

I wanted so bad to tell her that I was seventeen and wasn't about to be hit with no fucking belt, but I knew better. She would have mopped the floor with my ass if I even fixed my face to say some shit like that to her. After washing the dishes, I went into my room to start my homework that I could have been finished with if I didn't have to clean dishes that I didn't dirty. My cell rang. It was my best friend, Tamika, asking if I wanted to come chill with her for a little while, but I knew my mom wasn't trying to let me out on a school night. She convinced me to tell her that we were going to study for a test that we have tomorrow, so I told her that I would call her back.

Once I ended the call, I went back out to the living room, rolling my eyes instantly at the sight of my mother's boyfriend sitting on the couch. He had his feet up on the table, drinking a beer while watching television with his bum ass. He must have been in her room the entire time that she was fussing with me to clean the dishes and knowing his ass, he's probably the one that told her to leave them for me. I couldn't stand his non-working, sitting on his ass all day, lazy motherfucking bitch ass. I didn't even acknowledge him as I walked to my mother's bedroom to ask her if I could go to the next building and study with Tamika for about an hour.

"Katrina, it's going on five and if you're not back by six... I promise you... If I have to come looking for you, I'm going to beat your ass all the way home." she threatened but I didn't care as long as she said yes.

I rushed to the front door before she could change her mind, but before my hand touched the knob, she was calling my name.

"Yes." I answered annoyed.

Londyn

"Aren't you forgetting something?" She asked as I looked at her with a confused look on my face.

"How are you going to study with no books?" She asked with raised eyebrows.

"Oh, I forgot," I said, running to my room to retrieve my bookbag before leaving out the front door.

Tamika's building was right next door to mine, so it took me about a minute to get to her apartment that was located on the first floor.

"Hey girl! I thought you said that you were going to call me back," she said after answering the door.

"I know, but I wasn't waiting a minute longer in that place to give her a chance to change her mind. Anyway, what are we about to do because I damn sure didn't come to do homework like I told my mother I was," I said to her, laughing.

"Hell to the no if you thought I was about to do homework. I'm trying to go to building four to watch those niggas ball," she said excitedly. And I was just as excited, hoping to see Q's fine ass.

Q was like twenty-two and I knew that he didn't have eyes for my young ass, but it didn't stop me from drooling every

4

time I saw his fine ass. We left from Tamika's apartment and headed toward building four with me telling her to hurry because I only had like forty-five minutes left before having to be back home. My mother didn't play and meant every word that she said. She didn't have a problem coming out here and embarrassing me. If she would just give me some freedom, I wouldn't have to lie to her every chance that I got just to get out of the house from under her and her boyfriend.

As soon as we walked to the back of building four, there he was on the court balling with his boys who were just as fine as his ass; but I only had eyes for Q. Tamika was sweating his homeboy Malik, but we both knew that it was wishful thinking that they would ever look at us the same as we looked at them.

"Why the hell your young asses out here watching these grown men and drooling at the mouth?" Tierra said, causing her friends to laugh.

I don't know why they were acting like they were so much older than us just because all their asses were eighteen already. Tierra lived in my building and for the life of me, I didn't understand why she was always hating on me. She didn't really know me to not like me, but it never stopped her from putting energy into me like I did some shit to her. I believe it might have to do with the fact that she was jealous of me because her grown ass man of a boyfriend always has his eyes on me whenever he saw me.

"We're drooling the same way your man be drooling at my girl every time he sees her," Tamika clapped back, causing her friends laughter to cease.

"Bitch, please, my man would never look at her busted ass when he has all of this to look at," she said, standing and twirling around like she was the shit.

"So, let me ask you a question, Tierra, because I'm kind of confused. If my friend is this young busted female, why the fuck are you bothered? Why do you go out of your way to fuck with her every chance that you get? I'll tell you why you're bothered, it's because she doesn't have to cake her face with make-up, she doesn't have to wear the latest designer clothing to look good and she doesn't have to even look at your man to know that he's looking. She's flawless without even trying. That's why you're mad bitch!" Tamika barked.

"Bitch, I'll fuck your…" Tierra started before shots ranged out.

It was total chaos as everyone started running for cover, but I was frozen with fear as tears spilled from my eyes.

"Katrina, let's go!" Tamika yelled, getting my attention.

Giving My Heart to A Gangsta

I never been so scared in my life as I attempted to run towards her but failed miserably as I fell to my knees. I felt someone strong hands lift me up off the ground and when I looked up to see that it was Q, I was mesmerized, forgetting that I needed to continue running.

"You good, shorty?" He asked.

"Yeah, I'm good," I responded, voice shaking.

"Cool!" He belted before running to catch up with his boys as the sirens blared distinctly in the air letting him know they were close.

Tamika grabbed my hand as we continued running to the back door of building four, not stopping until we reached the front of the building.

"Girl, did you see Q fine ass help me up off the ground?" I panted, trying to catch my breath.

"Your silly ass was about to get shot, standing there like you have no damn sense," she laughed.

"I couldn't move, that's how scared I was when I heard the shots ring out," I told her.

Londyn

"You should be used to hearing gunshots because it's the fourth of July out this bitch just about every other night," she said.

"I know but I never been on the front line, so my ass couldn't move. Oh shit! What time is it?" I asked, forgetting that I was supposed to be back by six.

"It's six-thirty," she responded, causing me to gasp.

"Come on, Tamika. I have to get home," I said in a panicky voice.

I just pray that my mother wasn't out here looking for me, especially if she heard the gunshots. Once she sees my torn legging from falling, she's going to know that I wasn't at Tamika house. So again, I prayed.

"Girl, I'll call you if my mother doesn't put me in the hospital," I half joked as we parted ways.

I got like a few steps from my building and my heart stopped, seeing my mother walking towards me.

"Omg! Katrina, I was scared to death!" She cried, pulling me into her arms.

I wasn't expecting that from her but after she expressed how happy she was that I was ok, she cursed me out for not being where I said I was going to be. She grounded me for a week, but I wasn't tripping because I really scared her, so I deserved to be grounded. I went to bed that night thinking about Q and how he cared enough to stop and help me up off the ground, risking getting caught up.

I waited in front of my building for Tamika so that we could walk to the bus together when Tierra and her sidekick, Toya, walked out of the building.

"What was that fly shit you were talking yesterday?" She asked me when she knows that I didn't say shit to her ass.

Tamika was the confrontational one when I was the one that didn't feed into the bullshit unless you put your hands on me.

"Tierra, get out my face because you didn't hear me say shit to you. The only one bothered is your ass because I'm good over here," I told her, attempting to walk away from her miserable ass.

She should have been concentrating on passing the twelfth grade being her ass failed last year. The bitch about to be nineteen with her dumb ass, so that's where her focus should be instead of sweating me with her nonsense.

Londyn

"Bitch, why the fuck is you walking away when I'm talking to you?" She asked, pulling me back by my bookbag, causing me to almost lose my balance.

I took my bookbag off my back and swung on her ass, catching her dead in her face and causing her to stumble back. She rushed me, swinging wildly like a fucking white girl, so I started tagging that ass the way my uncles taught me. Once Toya saw her girl getting her ass kicked, she started punching me from behind, trying to help her friend cash a check she shouldn't of wrote. A crowd started to form and instead of someone breaking it up being these bitches was jumping me, they decided to record on their phones.

"Oh shit!" I heard someone say and I knew what that meant.

Tamika dragged Toya ass and that's when I continued to beat the breaks off Tierra's ass, giving her a reminder that she fucked with the wrong one. I don't fuck with this bitch, so I whooped her ass for every foul thing her ass ever said to me. My next-door neighbor, Mr. Roy, finally broke up the fight telling me to take my ass to school before he called my mother.

"I bet that bitch going to stop fucking with you now," Tamika laughed but I was pissed.

Chapter Two
(Katrina)

I wasn't about to go to school when my lip felt like it was starting to swell, and I could feel the burn from the scratches on my face.

"I'm not going to school like this." I said to Tamika.

"Well, let's go sit inside the Dunkin Donuts until my mother leaves for work, then we can go chill at my house," she suggested, and I agreed.

I knew my mother was probably going to receive that automatic attendance call, but I didn't care because I wasn't going to school. Just as we sat down at that small ass table in Dunkin Donuts, Q and Malik walked in with two females that I recognized from the neighborhood. I tried covering my face because of the evidence from the fight I just had, but Tamika kicked me under the table, causing me to say ouch rather loudly and drawing attention to myself.

"No school today?" Q asked.

Londyn

I just knew that I had to be dreaming or imagining things because it was no way this sexy man was talking to me.

"Nah, we're chilling," Tamika responded because I was stuck on stupid.

"So, your homegirl don't talk?" He asked her but looking at me.

Say something Katrina and stop acting like a scared little girl. He probably already thinks that you're young and you're proving him right, acting like you can't form a damn sentence. I thought to myself.

"I, I can talk," I stuttered, sounding dumb as hell.

"Really, Q?" One of the females he was with whined.

I could tell from his expression on his face that he was annoyed by her interrupting what he had going on over here.

"So, where the two of you chilling at?" He asked, ignoring her.

When Tamika gave him her address and apartment number, I gave her a look because she was bugging right now. I had butterflies in my stomach at the thought of them trying to chill with us, but I wasn't trying to get in trouble with Tamika for inviting guys older than us to her mom's apartment. Tamika

12

mother wasn't as strict as my mother, but I know that she wouldn't be happy with her inviting men into her house.

We been at Tamika house for about an hour, but Q and Malik were a no-show, making me realize that they were just fucking with us. *Why would they want to chill with two seventeen-year-old females?* I thought to myself, thinking about the two females that I saw them with earlier.

"Do you think that they're still coming?" I asked Tamika who already changed into some tight ass leggings and a tank with no bra on, with her hoe ass.

"Why wouldn't they come?" She asked sarcastically.

"Tamika, you do know that even if they come through, they only coming through to chill right? I don't think that they are looking at us on some 'get with' type shit. We have to keep in mind that Q and Malik are some block niggas making that paper that can have any female their own age," I reminded her.

"Fuck what you're talking about because *I may be young but I'm ready to sit on that nigga Malik dick and ride, ride,*" she sang, swaying her hips before dipping down and mimicking riding a dick, causing me to laugh at her crazy ass.

When I heard the knock on her door, my ass got nervous because I knew that it was them coming to chill like they said they would. I'm not going to front. When Q walked through the door, he had me feeling moisture between my legs because his swag meter was off the fucking chain.

Tamika, being the bold and aggressive one, took Malik by the hand, walking him down the hall to her bedroom and I was pissed. I wasn't ready to be left alone with Q because I didn't know what to say to his ass.

"Why are you acting shy?" He asked me after taking a seat on the couch.

"I'm not acting shy," I responded.

"What's your name? And how old are you?" He asked.

I know that he didn't know my age, but I at least thought that he knew my name; I guess not. I was wondering if I should tell him my real age or lie, but after thinking about it, I decided to tell him the truth. If he decided to leave after I told him that I was only seventeen, so be it, being I was stuck on the fact that he was interested in me that way anyway.

"My name is Katrina and I'll be eighteen in three months," I told him being honest.

"Seventeen, huh?" He questioned, pulling at his goatee and staring a hole through me.

Giving My Heart to A Gangsta

"Yes, seventeen. How old are you?" I asked even though I knew he was much older than me.

"I'm twenty-three, shorty; a grown ass man," he smiled.

"Well, I'm three months short of being a grown ass woman," I sassed, smiling at his ass.

"So, do you have a man?" He asked me just as we heard the headboard knocking from Tamika's bedroom, causing me to shake my head in embarrassment.

I prayed he didn't think that I was about to give up my goodies just because Tamika's hot ass decided to come up out of her panties.

"No, I don't have a man but that doesn't mean I'm about to get down like my friend," I told him, letting it be known.

"Shorty, I'm not pressed for no pussy. I just came to chill with you. And what happened to your face?" He finally asked.

"I had a fight earlier. That's why I didn't go to school today, because of my face," I told him.

"Shorty, you too pretty to be out here fighting, messing up that beautiful face of yours."

Damn, pretty and beautiful in one sentence. He had a bitch blushing hard as hell from his compliment.

15

Londyn

"Thank you and I wasn't trying to fight but this girl just keeps fucking with me because her boyfriend has a problem keeping his eyes in his head whenever he sees me," I admitted.

"Well, I can't blame a nigga for looking so you're probably going to have to fight a lot of bitches out here. A man would have to be blind not look at you," he flirted.

"So, do you have a girlfriend?" I asked him, curious if that girl from earlier was his girlfriend.

"Nah, I have a few chicks I rock with but not one of them can say that I'm their man," he said.

The thought of him entertaining other females had me feeling some way, but I should have known his fine ass was going to have a few females in his life.

"Do you have any children?" I wanted to know.

"Nah, I'm in these streets so I'm not trying to bring no children into this unpredictable life of mine right now," he admitted.

Malik and Tamika walked out of her room about an hour later and he wasted no time letting Q know that he was ready to go. I knew what that meant because I told Tamika time and time again that no nigga was going to want to fuck with her after giving up the panties so quick.

"I'm about to get up out of here but give me your number and I'll call you later," Q said to me, causing me to smile because he wanted to talk to me again.

"Malik, baby, don't you want my number?" Tamika purred.

"Nah, I'm good shorty," he said, causing her to frown when she saw that he was serious.

I felt bad, but she doesn't listen to me when I try to tell her that no nigga is trying to claim her when she keeps giving up the pussy. Malik ass hightailed out of the apartment like she burnt him or some shit, but Q gave me a hug and promised to call me later.

"You know that nigga not going to call you, right?" Tamika said.

I hated when she throws shade whenever her shit doesn't work out the way she wanted it to work out. I wanted to tell her that he was going to call because I wasn't quick with giving up my damn pussy like she was. Niggas will continue to fuck with you after giving up the pussy so quickly. They not trying to wife you, but she doesn't get that. She be mad at herself but like to take the shit out on me; I wasn't sticking around to hear it.

"It's time for me to go because it's almost that time and you know how my mother is," I said to her.

"Ok, call me later," she said, walking me to the door.

I had about ten minutes to kill before my mother expected me to be home, so I stopped at the corner store for a few snacks. Walking into my building, I prayed that my mother was in her bedroom and not the living room, but that prayer went out the window. She was walking down the hall when I entered my apartment which meant she was about to see my face. It wasn't too bad, but it was enough to know that I was in a fight or someone's cat attacked me.

"What happened to your face?"

"Remember I told you that Tierra from the 5th floor always got something smart to say because her man be looking at me? Well, yesterday she was calling me all kinds of names, but I ignored her. When I was leaving for school this morning, she approached me again. I tried walking away, but she pulled me by my bookbag, almost causing me to fall, so we started fighting. Her friend jumped in and they were jumping me until Tamika came and we all started fighting until Mr. Roy broke it up," I regretted telling her because she was taking off her house shoes and putting on her sneakers.

"So, these bitches want to jump my fucking baby," she ranted as she tied up her sneakers.

"Mom, Tamika and I handled it. You don't have to say anything; it's over." I tried to convince her, but I knew that it was no convincing her once her mind was made up.

While waiting for the elevator, I sent Tamika a text letting her know that my mother was about to go to Tierra house after seeing my face. Tamika text back with a lol, saying that she was on her way, causing me to shake my head and pray my mom didn't get locked up.

"Mom, you know if you go there with that bat in your hand, her mother's going to think that you came to fight and not talk," I said to her.

"Katrina, I don't give a flying fuck what her mother is going to think but I tell you what she's going to know. She's going to know that if her fucking cum sucking daughter come for my daughter again, I'm going to fuck her world up," she said talking crazy.

Londyn

I knew that my mother was a little crazy, but this right here was a bit much. She was about to fly off the handle after I already told her that it was over.

"Mom, why are you banging on the door like you the police?" I asked her.

When Tierra's mother opened the door, she looked at my mother and then she looked at the bat in her hand with a confused look on her face.

"What's going on, Cookie?" She asked, calling my mother by her nickname.

"Listen, I know we cool and shit but I'm going to tell you this one time and one time only, Sherita. Your fucking daughter got one more time to say something to my fucking daughter and I'm going to beat her ass like she's my child. Did you know that your daughter and her friend jumped my daughter this morning? I'm trying hard not to take this bat and go upside your fucking head with it right now because that's how fucking pissed I am. Don't nobody and I mean nobody fuck with my daughter when she's not fucking with them," she ranted, going about this the wrong way.

Giving My Heart to A Gangsta

"Tell your daughter stop being a hoe and I wouldn't have shit to say to her." Tierra came out of nowhere with the name calling again.

"Tierra!" Her mother shouted, but she didn't listen.

"Did your daughter tell you that every chance she gets, she be in my man face?" She lied, pissing me off.

"Stop lying Tierra because you know that I never said two words to your ugly ass boyfriend," I spat. She charged me and all hell broke loose.

Before she could get to me, my mother grabbed her ass and that's when Tierra's mother went to put hands on my mother. She made the biggest mistake of her life by doing that because my mother went Mayweather on her ass. Tierra went to jump in to help her mother. I yanked her ass back by her hair and we started fighting. The bitch tried to scratch my eyes out, pissing me off even more. So now I was in kill mode, but my fist never connected with her face because I was being pulled off her. When I saw Malik pulling my mother up off Tierra's mother, I knew that it was Q who saved that bitch life. I was so embarrassed and not just because he saw me fighting like a hood rat, but it seemed as if the whole fucking fifth floor was in the hallway watching. I turned to see Tamika's ass coming out of the stairwell all out of breath, letting me know that she ran up the stairs. Whenever the dope boys had business in the building, they would hold the elevator on that floor until they were done with business.

Tierra and her mother were still talking shit about how it wasn't over like they both didn't just get fucked up. My mother was now taking the bat to her door like a crazy woman, so I had to pull her away, telling her to go before the cops came.

"I told you about fighting and now I see why you didn't answer your phone," Q whispered while my mother was venting to Tamika. "I have to get up out of here because you and your mom just made it hot, but I'll call you back in a few," he said before him and Malik disappeared into the stairwell.

Chapter Three
(Tamika)

"Girl, your mother ain't no joke," I said to Katrina once we were in her apartment.

"Even though she took the bat with her, I still didn't think it was going to go that far. You know her and Tierra mom be chilling, so I didn't expect her to beat her ass like that," Katrina sighed.

"Well, that's what those bitches get. But enough about them. What was Q whispering in your ear?" I asked her.

"Oh, you peeped that?" She giggled.

"Yep, I don't miss a beat bitch. Now spill it," I told her, waiting for the tea.

"Nothing to tell, he just said that he told me about fighting, messing up my pretty face and that he called me," she smiled.

"Nah, he said more than that because your ass was smiling from ear to ear bitch. Did you see Malik ass act like he didn't know me?" I asked her.

23

"He was too busy trying to get my crazy mama off Tierra's mom," she laughed but she knew that nigga was avoiding me like I was a damn bill collector.

"He trying to play me, but it's all good. I'm about to go home and help my mother finish up dinner. I told her that I was going to the store, so I'll hit you up later," I told her.

"Ok, later," she said, walking me out.

When I got back to my apartment, I went to my room trying to figure out why every time I'm feeling a nigga, I rush to give up pussy knowing I'm going to get played after. I really like Malik, so I figured giving him some, he would see just how much I liked him. But, all it did was make him think that I'm a hoe. He doesn't want anything to do with me and he hurt my feelings not acknowledging me the same way Q acknowledged Katrina when he saw me earlier. I don't be trying to hate on her, but I get so tired of niggas wanting to be with her, whether she gives it up or not. I been crushing on Malik since last year, so for him to walk through my front door had me feeling like I hit the lottery or some shit. His dick game was fire and he had me begging him not to stop; that's how good it felt. During sex, I felt that he was feeling the same way I was feeling about him because he cared enough to keep asking me if I was ok and he kissed me so passionately. What man do you know that kiss like that if they had no plans on sticking around? I guess I read him wrong. My phone rang, and it was Katrina, taking me from my thoughts and me wallowing in my pity party.

"Hey, what's up?" I asked her.

"Girl, Q just called, and he wants me to take a ride with him!" She screamed into the phone.

A twinge off jealousy tried to rear its ugly head, but I shook it off because she was my girl and I didn't want to be *that girl*.

"So, why are you on the phone with me?!" I screeched into the phone.

"I'm trying to come up with an excuse to get out of the house," she responded.

"Just tell her that you're going to the corner store," I suggested.

"If I tell her that I'm going to the corner the store, that excuse will only buy me five minutes. What you think she's going to do to me when I get back hours later?" She whined.

"So, you trying to be out with him for hours?" I questioned.

Londyn

"No, silly, but it's going to take longer than five minutes," she laughed.

"I'm going to have my mother call your mother to ask her if you could go with me to the laundromat. I'm only doing this because I love your ass," I told her.

"Aww. Thanks girl. I owe you one."

"Yes, you do because I wasn't trying to do this laundry until this weekend. Anyway, when you get back, make sure you call to tell me everything."

"I promise," she said, ending the call.

Katrina was seventeen just like me, but her mom had her on a short leash and she didn't even have a curfew. I think it has to do with her brother being killed last year because ever since it happened, she was even more over protective about Katrina. She's always been overprotective but now she's overkill with it; always worrying that something is going to happen to her. I understood her fear, but she needed to let her live. If something was going to happen, she couldn't stop it. Something could happen on the way to school, during school or afterschool, so she really needed to ease up.

After my mom made the call, I grabbed the shopping cart and loaded it with my bag of dirty clothes, making my way out the door. Just as I was walking out of the building, I saw Katrina climbing inside of Q's Altima, causing that twinge of jealousy again. At the same time, I was happy for her. As soon as I walked into the laundromat, I regretted having to do it today when I saw that my classmate Aaron was also washing his clothes. Aaron had a crush on me, but I didn't see him in that way. He was cool, but not my type. As you can see, his ass up in here doing laundry too.

"Hey, Tamika," he smiled.

"What's up, Aaron?" I responded, keeping it moving, trying to find a washer nowhere near his ass.

I started taking my bag out of the shopping cart and he came over to assist me, causing me to roll my eyes in the back of my head. After he took the bag out of the cart, I thanked him, wanting him to take his ass back to washing his clothes and reading his book that he had in his hand when I walked in.

"Hey, if you're not busy afterschool tomorrow, how about you come over and chill with me?" He insisted on talking to me.

"I'm babysitting my baby cousin tomorrow afterschool," I lied.

Londyn

"Will you be babysitting the weekend too?" He asked with his persistent ass.

"I'm not sure. I just know that I'll have her tomorrow afterschool," I told him as I put my clothes into the washer.

"Here," he said, handing me quarters to start my washer that I kindly accepted.

"Thank you."

"You're welcome, Tamika," he smiled, walking back to his clothes and putting them in the dryer.

He was kind of cute; a nerdy kind of cute but again, he wasn't my type. So, he needed to try hooking up with one of those girls on his debate team.

"Tamika," he called out, causing me to suck my teeth as I walked over to him.

"Since you can't chill with me tomorrow, come let me whoop your ass in some Ms. Pac-Man," he said, surprising me because he almost sounded like he had a little thug in him.

"Trust me, this ain't what you want. I have Ms. Pac-Man on my phone and in my room. My mother got me the connect and play from Walmart. I be up all night playing and I'm good," I bragged.

Giving My Heart to A Gangsta

"You care to put a wager on it?" He questioned with a smile on his face.

"I don't have any money," I told him.

"You don't need any money. If I win, you have to agree to chill with me on Saturday for at least an hour."

"And if I win?" I asked with raised eyebrows.

"If you win, I'll take you to see the new Jumanji movie," he said.

"Bet," I said.

He popped in two quarters thinking he was slick. He knew that he wins either way because he still gets to be in my presence.

I was very competitive, and my ass was copping an attitude because he was kicking my ass and smiling while doing so. My wrist was on fire, but I didn't care. I was determined to beat him, but he was the king of Ms. Pac-Man, so I had to hang out with his ass on Saturday.

He finished up with his clothes, telling me he would see me on Saturday before leaving out of the laundromat with a big ass smile on his face. When I left the laundromat, all I wanted to do was go home, eat my dinner, shower and go to bed, but

Londyn

Katrina had other plans. She kept me on the phone for about an hour, telling me about her and Q's outing. This time, I was jealous at all he was doing, and he just met her. She said that he took her to get something to eat and when he saw her phone, he upgraded her to an iPhone when he didn't even hit yet. I wanted an iPhone now that my best friend has one, but my ass couldn't afford one. My mother damn sure wasn't going to spend that kind of money on no cell phone. She said that he was taking her to see the new Jumanji movie on Saturday. I told her about Aaron and how I would have been going if I won the game. She said that I should tell him that I still wanted to go so that we could all go together, but I don't know what planet she was living on. Q wasn't trying to hang out with Aaron's nerdy ass, let alone go on a double outing with him. I told her that I would see her in the morning in front of her building, but she told me that Q was going to pick her up and drop her off to school. He must have already been feeling her if he got her a new phone and now he was personally coming to pick her up to take her to school. I told her that I would see her at school tomorrow before ending the call.

When I exited the building the next morning, Q's car was in front of my building with Katrina hanging out the passenger side window yelling that it took me long enough to come downstairs.

"You were waiting on me?" I asked, confused because she said she had a ride last night.

"Yes, you know I wasn't going to have a ride and have my girl taking the bus. Get in," she smiled.

"What's up, Q? Thanks for the ride," I said, getting comfortable enjoying the feel of his leather seats.

"No problem, shorty," he responded.

When we pulled up in front of the school, Katrina sucked her teeth, causing me to look at what she was looking at. Tierra was standing in front of the school with like five girls, probably waiting on us.

"What's up?" Q asked.

"I'm so tired of fighting this bitch when I'm not even checking for her man," Katrina told him.

He didn't say anything as he got out of the car. So, we got out following behind him, ready for whatever at this point. If Tierra thought she was going to jump my friend, that bitch was sadly mistaken.

Londyn

"Tierra, let me holla at you," Q said to her and she walked over with a big ass smile on her face.

"What's up, Q baby?" She flirted.

"Yo, check this out. I don't know what beef you have with Katrina, but you need to fall back. She's my girl and anybody that fucks with my girl fucks with me. You already know how I get down. And the same shit goes for her girl, Tamika. Fuck with her, you're fucking with me," he barked, erasing that big ass smile she had on her face.

"You didn't have to do that, Q. I'm not scared of that girl or her flunkies," Katrina said to him.

"Fuck that shit. She's not going to keep fucking with you for no reason, trying to fuck up your face to look like hers," he laughed.

"Anyway, thanks for the ride," she told him before we left to get to class.

"Girl, did you hear him call me his girl?" She gloated.

"Yes, I heard him." I rolled my eyes, causing us both to laugh as we walked to class.

Katrina and I parted ways after third period because we didn't have fourth period together, so I stopped at my locker

Giving My Heart to A Gangsta

before going to class. I needed to grab my notebook for my history class and to get my lunch money from my bag since lunch was next period. Aaron approached me at my locker, asking for my number so that he could call me tomorrow to find out what time I wanted to come chill. I forgot about chilling with him that fast as I gave him my number.

Chapter Four
(Quentin)

"Nigga, you bugged out for buying that bitch a fucking iPhone. She's probably a hoe just like her fucking homegirl," Malik clowned.

"She's not a hoe nigga, so watch your fucking mouth!" I barked at his ass.

"Oh shit! She put that young pussy on his ass and got him in here ready to kill for her ass," he said, putting his hands up in surrender.

"Fuck you. What's up with this money?" I changed the subject.

I been kicking it with shorty for about a month now and she still didn't come up off the pussy, but I wasn't going to tell his ass that. He'll really be clowning a nigga if he knows I didn't get the pussy and buying her shit, but that was his dumb mentality. He was calling her homegirl a hoe for fucking him the same day she met him, but Katrina told me that her girl been feeling him for a good minute. So, she didn't fuck him because she's a hoe. She fucked him because she like his stupid ass, but he said fuck her and is on to the next already. Katrina and I aren't exclusive yet because she's younger than me, but I'm feeling the shit out of her. She's going to be eighteen in two more months, so we just chilling right now. So, I'm still doing my thing with a few other females. Malik ass shouldn't have taken the pussy, even if she was willing, knowing her ass wasn't eighteen yet.

"Everybody count was on point except that nigga Troy, who shit came up short last week too," Malik responded, bringing me back to business.

"So, what the fuck he saying about his count being short? And how the fuck is it being handled?" I wanted to know.

If a nigga come up short one time, I probably would let the shit slide. But if it happened a second time, his ass needed to be handled.

"Ebay been looking for that nigga for a week now, but he's MIA," he said, pissing me off.

"So, how much this nigga came up short?" I asked him.

"He was short a G the first week and his count was short by almost two G's this week."

Londyn

That was chump change to a nigga like me, but that nigga needed to be made an example of how not to play with my fucking money. If Ebay gave his ass a pass the first time, that nigga should have been making sure his count was right the next time. Being his count wasn't on point this week meant to me that he didn't give a fuck about how I was going to feel, so it was time that I pay his ass a visit. Niggas see that I be on some chill shit, so they want to test my gangsta. I guess it was time to make believers out of these motherfuckers again. I grabbed my pistol, put it in my waist and told Malik ass to get up because we were riding out. This nigga Troy was out here playing hide and seek with Ebay's ass, but I wasn't about the games. He wanted to hide, so I was going to seek his ass the only way I knew how.

We pulled up to Astoria Houses where I knew his girl stayed. I was about to get that nigga to come to me. Malik knocked on the door and as soon as that bitch opened the door, I hit her ass in the face, causing her to stumble back into the apartment. Her son was sitting on the floor playing with a truck, but I didn't give a fuck. I didn't like putting my hands on a female, but I was here about business. I needed to prove to that nigga that just like he didn't give a fuck about my money, I didn't give a fuck about busting his bitch shit open.

Giving My Heart to A Gangsta

"Get that nigga Troy on the phone now, bitch!" I barked.

"Can I please take my son to the other room?" She cried.

"Bitch, if you don't get Troy on the phone right now, your son is going to be the least of your worries," I told her ass.

Malik walked back into the living room after checking the apartment and making sure that nigga wasn't already here. As soon as I heard Troy's voice, I snatched the phone from her, pushing her down to the floor.

"Bitch nigga, you got fifteen minutes to make it to your girl crib before I put a bullet in her fucking head!" I barked into the phone.

"Who the fuck is this?" His punk ass asked, trying to sound tough.

"It's the grim reaper here to fucking collect, so you decide if it's your bitch life or yours," I growled before ending the call.

This nigga walked in the door on some Tony the Tiger tough guy shit but knew his ass wasn't about that life. Let a nigga call me telling me to get home before they kill my girl. Trust I'm walking in this bitch guns blazing. His ass went to say something, but I silenced his ass with two to the fucking head, silencing his ass for life. His bitch was screaming but I silenced her ass by pointing the gun in her face. I told her that if she said anything, I was going to come back and kill her ass too before walking up out of that dirty ass apartment.

"Damn, I didn't know you was going to kill that nigga?" Malik said.

"So, you thought I was coming to talk to this nigga after he let the shit happen more than once? You know me better than that. You can let it be known to every motherfucker that works for me, if they come up short, there will be consequences. Let Ebay know that he needs to holla at me asap," I told him.

Ebay is cool peoples who I been rocking with since high school; but if this nigga didn't know how to run his crew, maybe his ass needed to be demoted. We clicked in high school because he was a hustler by nature and that's how he got his name. He was always selling some shit.

I dropped Malik back off to his car before leaving to go home to shower and change my clothes since I was taking Katrina out. We been going out every weekend, so this weekend wasn't any different because I enjoyed spending time with her. She was on a short leash with her mom, so she had to get creative when getting permission to leave the house. I thought it was a bit extreme being she was seventeen, but she told me that her mother worried about her after her brother was killed last year. I understand how her mother is feeling, but if she's with me she wouldn't have to worry. Still, she can't even tell her mother about me. She said that once she turns eighteen, that's when she'll introduce me to her mother. So until then, she has to keep telling her that she's at Tamika place.

I called Katrina to let her know that I was downstairs, and she told me to pull up in front of her girl's building. I guess she left out of her house and headed over to Tamika's being I'm sure that's where she told her mom she was going to be. Malik was having a get together at his crib, so that's where we were headed. I didn't tell her that since she didn't like being around a lot of people. I knew it had to do with the age difference, but I told her not to sweat what nobody thought or said about it. She came out of Tamika's building looking hood cute because I hooked her up with the new Jordan's that just came out, some black Levi's and a black North Face down jacket. So, I guess that's the reason she was at Tamika crib. She had to change her clothes because if her mother saw what she was wearing, she would have had some explaining to do.

"You look cute," I told her once she was in the car.

"Thanks to you," she smiled.

Londyn

"Anything for you, shorty," I told her, pulling out.

When we pulled up to Malik's spot about twenty minutes later, I saw the look on her face and knew that she wasn't going to want to be here.

"Where are we?" She frowned when she saw that I turned the car off.

"This is Malik's spot. He's having a few people over to chill but don't worry, it's cool," I said to her.

"I hope so," she sighed, getting out of the car.

"What's up my nigga?" Malik greeted, letting us in.

"Hey, Katrina," he acknowledged.

I didn't know that he was going to have all these damn people here because I wouldn't have come with Katrina. I could tell that she was already uncomfortable because niggas were drinking and passing the blunt around. This wasn't her scene, but she didn't say anything as she took a seat on the couch, removing her jacket. I told her that I was going to get something to drink and asked her if she wanted a drink, but she declined. I knew that she wasn't of legal age to be drinking but it would have calmed her nerves, I thought as I walked over to the table to fix me a drink.

40

Giving My Heart to A Gangsta

"So, you're on babysitting detail tonight?" Jemima tried to clown.

Her ass was just mad because I smashed and dashed on her hoe ass. Now she was in her fucking feelings.

"Jemima, move around and stop being on bullshit," I barked.

"So, it's like that, Q?" She asked like she didn't just try to clown a nigga.

"You came at a nigga on some bullshit being petty, so yeah it's like that," I told her, walking away from her trick ass.

"I take it she's one of your groupies," Katrina said when I finally made it back to where she was sitting.

"Nah, that trick on some bullshit," I said, leaving it at that because she didn't need to know that Jemima was mad because I didn't want to fuck with her.

"She's mad because you're here with me and probably wondering why you would pick me instead of someone your own age, right? I'm not going to lie but I be wondering the same thing too," she admitted.

"Katrina, I told you about sweating the small shit. If I wanted to be with her or anyone else for that matter, trust, you wouldn't be the one sitting here. Now lighten up and let's have some fun with the rest of these niggas," I told her, shutting that insecurity shit down.

"Yo, nigga. I know you're not going to sit on the couch all damn night," Malik ass said before passing me the blunt.

I hit the blunt taking a few pulls before passing it back to his ass, contemplating if I should leave her or not. His ass wanted me to kick it with him and the homies in the game room, but it wouldn't be a good look being she was still uncomfortable. When she looked up at me with a smile on her face telling me to go and that she would be ok, I left to go kick Malik's ass in some pool. I didn't realize that I left Katrina for like an hour. To my surprise, she had a smile on her face as she was interacting with a few of the other females. Jemima was standing across the room shooting daggers in her direction with her hating ass.

"Excuse me, ladies," I said to them, pulling Katrina up and telling her that we were leaving.

It was getting late and I knew that she had to be back home before her mother started to worry and call or go to Tamika's crib.

Giving My Heart to A Gangsta

"You know we didn't have to leave," she said once we were outside.

"It's getting late and I know that your mother probably would be worrying soon if you don't walk through the door," I told her.

"She's letting me spend the night with Tamika and her mother tonight so she's not expecting me home until the morning. Tamika's mother is working the night shift tonight so she's not going to know that I didn't spend the night."

"So, does that mean you chilling with a nigga at his crib tonight?" I asked her.

"That's what it means," she said, doing some little girlish dance being silly and causing me to crack up at her ass.

We stopped at Wild Wings to get something to eat before heading to my crib. Malik had all that fucking liquor but no food. We laid up watching movies after eating and I was trying hard to be on my best behavior knowing she wasn't of age yet. It was hard. She must have been feeling something too because she turned looking up at me with lust in her eyes as she kissed my lips. She was going to be eighteen in two months, so I said fuck it as I returned her kiss, sticking my tongue in her mouth. I don't know what happened because the nigga in me wanted to

Londyn

fuck the shit out of her but being she wasn't a jump-off, I just held her until we both fell asleep.

Chapter Five
(Katrina)

"So, all he did was kiss you?" Tamika asked.

"Yep, all he did was kiss me," I responded in a disappointed tone.

"Katrina, that must mean he cares enough to wait, unlike these other niggas out here," she tried to convince me.

"Anyway, you never told me about how things went with you and Aaron," I changed the subject.

"Girl, you been hanging out with Q so much that we don't talk like we used to, so it slipped my mind. Let me tell you, when I say you can't judge a book by its cover... girl, you really shouldn't because this nigga was nothing like we thought. All this time we were thinking that he was a nerd because he was on the debate team and all his friends were a part of the geek squad, but nope; he's far from a nerd. He called my phone and told me to come downstairs. When I got downstairs, I swear my voice got caught in my throat. This nigga had a fresh fade wearing an Alvin Kamara jersey and some black jeans with some Nubuck Timbs looking fly ass shit. So, I walked ahead of him in the direction towards the building that we thought he lived in, but he stopped me. He took my hand and walked me over to a black Lexus, opening the door and letting me in. I was bugging like who the fuck is this nigga and what did he do with Aaron's nerdy ass," she laughed.

"So, he doesn't live up the street and he drive a Lexus?" I asked, confused.

"Hell no, he doesn't live up the street. That's his grandmother's apartment and he come every day afterschool to help her out before heading home," she said.

"So, did you give him some?" I asked, praying she said that she didn't.

"Nope, we played video games and watched movies until he drove me home. He was a gentleman and I'm not going to lie, I enjoyed his company. Not once did I feel like I had to give him some pussy just to see him again," she admitted.

"I'm happy for you, Tamika. I hated that you felt you had to sleep with these dog niggas to keep one. All you had to do was wait for the right man to come along and show you different," I preached.

Giving My Heart to A Gangsta

"So, bitch, your birthday is next week. Any plans?" She reminded me.

"No, my mother will probably bake a cake like she does every year, but that's about it," I said sadly.

"I'm sure Q is going to do something for you," she stated, causing me to smile.

I never cared too much about my birthday because my mother couldn't afford to do more than what she does. So, it was just another day, honestly. I was just a little excited to see what Q was going to get me being he already got me a new phone, sneakers, jeans and a jacket. Tamika was trying to get me to cut school on my birthday, but I told her that I had a test in history, which was a lie. I just loved all the happy birthday wishes that I got throughout the day because it made me feel special, even if it was for one day. I left Tamika's apartment to go home when Aaron called telling her that he wanted to take her to get something to eat. She invited me along, but I declined. As soon as I got off the elevator, my phone alerted me that I had a text message.

Q- Wyd?

Me- Just about to walk inside of my apartment. What's up?

Londyn

Q- Don't go inside. I'll be in front of your building in like five minutes.

Me- Ok.

I walked back over to the elevator pressing the button, praying that my mom or her loser boyfriend didn't open the door and see me getting back on the elevator. I pressed the button to the lobby going down, but it stopped on the fifth floor. When Tierra and the girl from Malik's get together got on the elevator together, I sucked my teeth.

"I see that nigga Q upgraded this bum bitch," she said to Tierra and they both laughed.

I wasn't about to feed into the bullshit because she was just mad that Q didn't want her skinny ugly ass. I prayed that the elevator got to the lobby so that I could go about my business and away from their miserable asses.

"Did Q tell you that he was at my house the night before that get together at Malik house? I bet he didn't tell you that he had me bent over my kitchen table fucking the shit out of me," she taunted.

When the elevator made it to the lobby this bitch must have been big mad because I didn't say shit, so she pushed me trying to get a reaction out of me. As much as I wanted to swing on this bitch, I kept it moving knowing that Q was on his way or already out front waiting on me. I knew her seeing me get into his car was enough to wipe that smirk off her face, but this bitch just wouldn't stop. When I opened the lobby door, this time she kicked me in my back, causing me to fall face first. I don't know how the hell I got up off the ground that fast, but I felt like the hulk as I jumped on her ass, knocking her to the ground. I wanted to stomp her ass while she was down, but I wanted her to know that she couldn't beat me, so I gave her the opportunity to get back up. As soon as she got up and charged at me, I knocked this bitch right back down and she fell hard this time. I expected Tierra to jump in, but I guess she was tired of getting her ass beat or scared of what Q said to her ass. When the bitch got back up, a resident pushed her into the building, saving her from getting that ass tapped again. When I walked down the ramp, I saw why Tierra didn't jump in. Q was standing against his car watching the fight with a smirk on his face.

"You good?" He asked, pulling me in for a hug.

"I'm good, just tired of these bitches trying me," I said, fighting back tears.

I was pissed because I just wanted to be left alone before I really hurt one of those troublemaking, messy bitches.

Londyn

"Don't cry, shorty. I'm going to handle it," he said, opening the passenger side door for me.

"Where are we going?" I asked him. If it had anything to do with his friends, I wanted no parts of it.

"We're going back to my crib to chill if that's ok?" He asked.

"Ok," I told him.

He wanted to stop for something to eat but I told him that I wasn't hungry because a bitch was still in her feelings. I was at the point that I was going to tell him that I couldn't see him anymore. I went from having no fights to like three in one week. I swear, if I ever have a daughter, I'm going to drill in her head that if a man doesn't want you it's his loss and to move on. It doesn't make no sense to be out here trying to fight other females that he does want just to be looking stupid out here in these streets. When we finally got to his house and I went to the bathroom, the tears fell after seeing my forehead fucked up from the fall. I stood in that mirror counting to ten to calm myself down because I wanted to murder a bitch right now. If my mother saw my face looking crazy again, she's really going to want to murder someone, so I was going to have to lie. I just hoped that no one tells her that they saw me outside fighting because this shit is getting ridiculous. I lived in the projects all my life and never had to fight. I was always able to ignore the bullying from Tierra. We were cool until she started dating Karim from building four, who couldn't keep his eyes off me whenever he saw me. I understood her being upset but she needed to check her man when she knows that I'm not checking for his ass. I've only been crushing on one man and that man was Q. And she knows that because, like I said, we used to be cool. Her mother was always at my house chilling with my mother and that's how my mother met that loser boyfriend of hers. He was a friend of Tierra's mother's boyfriend. She hooked them up and they been together since. I find hard to believe she stayed with this bum for so long.

"Are you ok in there?" Q asked through the door.

"I'm ok," I responded as I looked in his medicine cabinet for something to clean my face with but didn't find anything.

Coming out of the bathroom, he was standing there with peroxide and cotton balls in his hand, causing me to smile. After cleaning up my face it really didn't look much better because of some of my missing skin from the scrape. I knew that I was going to need some Palmers coco butter to rub on it every day until my skin comes back. I'm praying that this isn't going to be a permanent scar because I'm too pretty for this bullshit.

"Can I ask you a question?" I asked him.

"What's up?"

"That girl that I was fighting said that you were at her house the night before we went to Malik's place. Is it true?" I wanted to know.

"Yeah, that's why that trick was mad when I showed up with you," he responded casually.

"So, you go to her house and fuck her, then show up to Malik's house with me and she's the trick?" I said, shaking my head.

I wasn't defending her but how dare he call her a trick when he's the one that led her to believe they were dealing with each other, just to show up with me the next day. I know if I just slept with a dude and he show up the next day with another female, my ass is going to be pissed off too. I wouldn't take it out on the other female, but I would be having a million and one questions for his ass.

"So, are you calling me a trick?"

Giving My Heart to A Gangsta

"I'm just saying it's not a good look to be fucking a bitch the night before and show up with another female in her face the next day. I understand why she was mad now, but she still shouldn't have taken it out on me. I wasn't the one that fucked her," I told him, feeling myself getting upset.

I was upset because, although we didn't make us official, he was still seeing me every day like we were together. So, I felt a way about him fucking someone else.

"Listen, I could have sat here and told you that she was lying but I told you the truth," he said like that made me feel any better.

Niggas be acting like they can't go without pussy and the shit disgusted me because he knows that I'm feeling him. He literally had to wait a couple of weeks to be intimate with me, being it seemed as that's why he wasn't trying to sleep with me. But then again, I couldn't be mad because we weren't together, but it did give me something to think about.

"I appreciate you being honest, but I still don't understand why you felt the need to sleep with someone else while seeing me," I told him.

"You wouldn't understand because you're not a man."

Londyn

"So, do you care to explain what my not being a man has to do with your urgency of getting pussy instead of waiting on me?" I asked, causing him to sigh like he wasn't expecting me to question his comment.

I didn't want to get into an argument with him about it, but I wanted him to explain his comment to me. I get confused as to why men can fix their face to degrade a woman by calling her a trick or a hoe but still lay down with her. I asked him if she was one of his groupies and he clearly said no and that she was on some bullshit; never saying she was on bullshit because of his fucking actions. He did tell me that he was rocking with a few females, but I just figured that once we started hanging tight, he would have cut their asses off.

"All I'm saying is that men have needs and it's not like I didn't tell you that I was still rocking with a few chicks."

"You did but I just thought that once we started kicking it, you wouldn't need to still be rocking with other females. So, at what point will you no longer be rocking with other females?" I asked him.

"I fucked around with her that night, but I haven't been rocking with anyone but you. If it makes you feel any better, I promise you that my monster stays in my pants unless I'm pulling it out for you."

It didn't make me feel any better, but I decided to leave it at that being he isn't my man.

Chapter Six
(Katrina)

"Happy birthday to you, happy birthday to you, happy birthday Katrina, happy birthday to you," my mother sang, waking me up out of my sleep.

When I opened my eyes, she was standing there holding three balloons with the words *happy birthday* written on them and a gift in her hand. Now mind you, my mother has never given me a gift passed the age of ten, so this was an epic moment right now. I got up hugging her tight, almost knocking her down. That's how happy I was to be getting a gift.

"Katrina, you didn't even open the gift yet," she laughed.

"I'm so happy right now," I told her, taking the gift from her hand.

When she handed me the gift bag that I didn't even notice, I felt like a kid on Christmas morning running downstairs to a tree filled with presents. I opened the first box that she had in her hand, ripping the paper so fast because I was excited to see what was inside. When I saw that it was two pairs of seven jeans, two polo sweaters and a few pairs of the stripped knee-hi socks that I love to wear, I was happy as shit. I was in awe and when I opened the big ass gift bag that she had and saw the Ugg box. I started jumping up and down praying that they were the ones that I always wanted. She could never afford them so when I opened that box and saw that they were the ones I always wanted, I almost cried.

"Mom, thank you so much for making this the best birthday ever," I told her.

I don't know where she got the money to get me such expensive gifts, but I was more than grateful the same way I would have been if she only baked me a cake like she's done every year.

"You're welcome baby and just keep in mind that those presents are your birthday and graduation present," she laughed.

"Well, being its only December 8th, I still have to get something for Christmas," I reminded her with a smile.

"I don't know how I skipped over Christmas. Anyway, don't forget to read the card," she said before leaving out my room to start breakfast.

Londyn

I don't know what had gotten into my mother, but I wasn't complaining. I thought as I took the card from the bag to read it.

Katrina, we both know that I haven't been the best parent and I want to change that because I've missed out on so much of your life. When we lost Trey, I honestly believed that I lost myself and became a woman that you no longer recognized. I know that my being overprotective has become overbearing so much so that I've made you feel as if you were being punished for something that you weren't doing. When I saw your face the other day, it made me realize that I had no idea what you were dealing with because I don't talk to you anymore. This gift isn't a deal breaker, it's merely a gift that you deserve for always being respectful when at times I didn't deserve respect. I'm sorry and thank you for loving me unconditionally.

When I tell you, I cried after reading the card; I cried. I cried one of those heaving up and down cries that you have after getting a big mama beating. When I got out of the shower, I put on the red polo sweater with the black seven jeans and of course, my new Uggs. My mom had it smelling so good in here that she had my stomach growling and I couldn't wait to dig in. When I walked into the kitchen, Tamika's ass was sitting at the table with a big ass smile on her face. She came bearing gifts and more balloons like she did every year. She got me a big ass teddy bear holding a frame with a picture of both of us. I remember that picture well because it was taken at Coney Island the summer that just past with *best friends forever* written on the top. That gift may not have meant a lot to anybody else, but I loved it and his big ass was going to sit right in the corner of my room. I gave them both a hug for making my birthday special. So special that I didn't need validation of my day from classmates and teachers that I always looked forward to every year. After breakfast, Tamika and I left out for school. When we exited the building, Q was standing against his car waiting on us.

"Girl, I'll see you later. Enjoy your birthday," Tamika said, giving me a hug.

"What are you talking about you'll see me later? You not going to school?" I asked her.

"I'm going to school, but you're not," she smirked, running off towards Aaron who I didn't even see standing there.

I walked over to Q who was now standing there with a big ass smile on his face, looking at me like I was his midnight snack causing me to smile with his ass.

Londyn

"Happy birthday, shorty," he said, pulling me into his arms and tonguing me down right there in front of my building.

I just turned eighteen, so I was like fuck it and tongued his ass back until he grabbed my ass and I had to stop him. If my mom walked out of the building, she wouldn't have cared about my turning eighteen. She would have fucked both of us up.

"You ready?" He asked me.

"Yeah, I'm ready because you're about to have me missing my first period," I said, but he just smirked and that's when I knew something was up.

"What aren't you telling me, Q?"

"Just get in and enjoy the ride shorty."

When I saw him get on the New Jersey turnpike, I started to panic. I didn't say anything but when I saw the sign telling him to merge onto I-80 W entering Pennsylvania, that's when I had to say something.

"Q, where are we going? There's no way that you're going to have me home by three-thirty."

"I have no plans of having you home until Sunday night," he said, causing me to gasp because he done lost his mind.

Giving My Heart to A Gangsta

"Have you lost your mind? You must be trying to get me killed, Q. I need for you to turn this car around right now," I said, getting so angry that I was on the verge of tears.

Just the thought of me not walking through that door afterschool and possibly giving my mother a heart attack was killing me inside. She already lost a child, so I wouldn't put her through the pain of not knowing where the hell I was or not knowing if I was coming back home.

"Calm down, I already spoke to your mother," he said, causing me to turn in my seat, waiting for him to explain.

"Listen, I hit up Aaron and got your girl Tamika's number because Malik's ass didn't have it and I told her that I wanted to talk to your mother. After she told me hell no I had to tell her my plans, that's when she gave me your mother's number. I told her that I wanted to speak to her about something concerning you, so she allowed me to come to the house being that you were still at school. I told her how I met you and how I respected the fact that you were only seventeen, letting it be known that we just been chilling. I let her know that I was feeling you and that I wanted to be with you. We got to talking and I have to say that your mom is cool and seemed to have lost her way. So, she expressed some shit and so did I. She told me how hard it's been on her, so I helped her out on some bills and gave her some money to get on her feet. I told her that I could get her a job at my uncle's construction site because he was looking for someone to work in the office. I also let her know the only way that I would get her the job is she had to leave that bum ass nigga alone."

Tears flooded my face and if he wasn't driving, I would have kissed him a million times because that's how grateful I felt right now. I was wondering where my mom got the money to get me such expensive gifts but brushed it off, figuring she might have hit the daily number. She was known to play the numbers when she was behind on a bill in hopes of hitting that number, so it wasn't too farfetched. I would have never expected him to have done this and he probably wouldn't have told me if I didn't look like I was about to have a panic attack.

"Thank you," I said, wiping my face.

"Anything for you, shorty. I told you that. Now wipe your face because today is your birthday. Nothing but smiles are allowed. Ok?"

"Ok," I told him wiping my face again, but the tears didn't want to stop.

I picked up my phone and sent my mom a text saying thank you because she didn't have to agree to him taking me away for my birthday. I know she probably was going to worry the entire time that I was going to be gone, so I was going to make sure to check in with her.

We pulled up to the cabin about forty-five minutes later and I was happy as shit to be in the Poconos for the weekend.

"Oh shit! Q, I have no clothes for this weekend getaway," I told him.

"Your mom packed your suitcase and it's in the trunk," he smiled.

"Come on. I'll get the suitcases later," he told me, pulling me towards the door.

When we walked through the door, I was in awe seeing that it was a lakefront through the big ass bay windows. It was big with a fire place in the front room that looked cozy as I imagined him making love to me in front of it. My thoughts were interrupted when the front door opened with Tamika and Aaron walking inside. I screamed like I saw a spider as I ran into her arms, hugging her before punching her in the arm for not telling me.

"Tamika was the deal breaker for your mother to agree to this trip," Q announced.

Londyn

"You damn right because my day one doesn't go anywhere without me," Tamika laughed.

"Well, we got two more guests coming so I suggest you and Aaron go up and pick a room. The master bedroom belongs to me and the birthday girl," he said to them, leaving me wondering who else he invited.

"Who else is coming?" I asked him.

"My boy Malik and whatever chick he decides to bring," he said like it was no big deal.

I was a bit disappointed because I would have rather spent my birthday with just the two of us, but I guess the more the merrier. Well, at least that's what they say.

Malik showed up with some chicken head named Nicola who was well known in the projects, but he had the nerve to curve my friend just to get with a hoe. I swear I see her ass with so many different dudes that you couldn't tell me that her ass wasn't tricking. If he could stick his dick in her, Tamika may have dodged a bullet because his ass was a damn hoe himself.

When Tamika came downstairs, she rolled her eyes at Malik causing them two to go at it like a damn divorced couple. I could do nothing but laugh at them because he's the one that kicked her to the curb. She accepted it and moved on, so I didn't understand what the beef was about.

"So, you here with that lame ass nigga?" He asked her. I was confused. Wasn't he the one that hit and quit?

"Lame? Have you looked in the mirror lately?" She laughed.

"What am I missing?" Nicola asked with attitude evident in her voice.

"No, you're not missing anything. What you're witnessing right now is a hating ass nigga," Tamika barked.

"Yo, chill with that shit on my baby birthday," Q told them both.

"Yeah because if you two need to release some of that built-up stress, take that shit to one of the bedrooms," I added, laughing my ass off.

"Malik, did the two of you used to date?" Nicola asked him.

"Don't ask me shit!" He barked, going to the bedroom and slamming the door.

Aaron came back inside carrying a crate with like six bottles of liquor and telling Q that he was going to need help bringing the food in. When they went outside, I pulled Tamika to the side to find out what the hell that shit was about with Malik.

"Tamika, what the hell was that between you and Malik?" I asked her, whispering.

"Girl, he's been tripping since I gave him the pussy again. Now he's in his feelings because I been hanging out with Aaron, but he shows up with this trick," she admitted.

"When the hell did this happen?" I asked because she never kept secrets from me before.

"We been fucking on the low for about two weeks now," she admitted with a smirk on her face.

"And you couldn't tell me?" I rolled my eyes, pretending to be mad, walking away from her ass.

Chapter Seven
(Tamika)

I couldn't believe that nigga had the balls to walk up in here with this two-dollar hoe and fix his face to question me. I was too through with his ass and should have walked away that day I saw him in Popeye's. I was going to get dinner for my mom and I. She was tired after work and didn't feel like cooking, so I ended up going to Popeye's. I was standing in line getting my order when someone tapped me on my shoulder trying to get my attention. When I turned around, it was him. I knew had he known it was me he wouldn't have even bothered, but all he saw was a fat ass and that's why he tapped me. I asked him why the hell he was touching me and that's when he started kicking game about how he was sorry and how he thought that I was out there which was bullshit. I honestly think that he was worried about what people was going to say. Seeing who he came here with, he couldn't be too worried about anybody knowing he's fucking with this hoe. Long story short, I fell for the nigga's apology and we been creeping almost every day since seeing each other in Popeye's. I know it sounds like I'm being stupid, but in my defense, I been feeling

67

his ass for a minute. So, it wasn't hard to forgive him but now I felt like cutting him and going upside that hoe head.

We were all having fun except Malik ass, who was sitting across the room with a mean mug on his face pissing me off. I didn't want Aaron to know that I had any dealings with his ass, but he was making it obvious that he wasn't happy that I was here with him. I'm sure that Q told him that Aaron and I were going to be here. That's probably why he snatched that hoe up who he isn't paying any attention too. I got up to go get some more orange juice for my drink and this nigga followed me into the kitchen like nobody was going to notice. I had this nigga gone off this pussy, now he up in here acting like a fucking baby looking for their pacifier to soothe them.

"Tamika, why the fuck you come here with this nigga?" He asked, causing me to sigh.

"Malik, don't do this shit right now? We are both here with someone else so let's talk about this another time," I told him.

"I don't give a fuck about that bitch!" He barked just as Aaron walked into the kitchen.

"Babe, you good?" He asked me but looking at Malik.

Giving My Heart to A Gangsta

"I'm good," I told him, grabbing his hand so that we could go back into the living room with the others.

Malik was really trying to get me caught up when he's not even my damn man. It's so funny how the tables turned. I been chasing his ass and now he's the one chasing because he sees that I'm not that person he thought I was. He was staring a hole through me, so I gave Q a look to tell him get his boy before he starts some shit up in here. All his ass did was laugh and pass the blunt. I wasn't amused by Malik's actions, so I tried my best to ignore him as I turned up the music. Nicola even mellowed out. He was the only one in his feelings right now with his hating ass. I had my drink in my hand while I danced in the middle of the floor with Katrina just trying to enjoy her birthday. Q got up and start dancing with her and Aaron got up and this nigga shocked me again because he could dance. I haven't slept with him yet but the way his dick was grinding into me... *Tonight might be the night,* I thought as I threw my ass into him.

"Aye, it's your birthday Katrina. Turn up, turn up," I laughed, hyping her up.

This chick is crazy. She had one leg between Q legs and doing the snake with her body and some new wind that I never saw before. She had us all falling out and when I say all, I mean Malik's ass too. I think he was starting to feel the effects of the blunt and the liquor. We were all dancing now and clowning at the same time. I needed to go to the bathroom because that liquor was sitting on my bladder. As soon as I walked out of the bathroom, Malik was standing there trying to be all up in my personal space, but I pushed him back. He pushed me up against the wall in the hallway, kissing me all over my neck and that's when I knew he was drunk.

"Let me just taste you," he said, tugging at my pants.

"Malik stop it! Aaron is downstairs, now move," I pushed him again.

I'm not going to lie and say that he didn't have a bitch wanting to feel his lips on my pussy, but I couldn't do that to Aaron. When I got back to the others and saw Aaron dancing with Nicola like he wasn't worrying about him having a bitch that could walk back in any minute, I went in search for Malik. Q and Katrina was in their own little world not paying that bitch who was dry humping the man I came with to even stop the shit.

Malik was coming out of the room he was staying in and I pushed his ass right back inside, locking the door.

Giving My Heart to A Gangsta

"You have five minutes," I told him stepping out of my pants and panties.

He had my right leg on his shoulder as I leaned up against the door, grabbing his head as he went to work on my pussy. I fucked his face until I released all my juices into his mouth and now this nigga wanted to hit the pussy, but I didn't know how much time we had. My mind was saying no but the liquor and how he had my pussy tingling was telling me yes, so I let him hit. When I walked back into the front room I didn't see Aaron or the hoe of the projects, so I was thinking that maybe he was doing me foul like I just done him. I felt guilty as hell when I walked into the kitchen and he was in there fixing me and him something to eat. I guess the dance was just an innocent dry fuck and he wasn't trying to fuck her. I fucked up, but I couldn't take the shit back. Q got up to get him and Katrina something to eat too so we were all just eating while the music played, and ESPN was on in the background until we heard arguing. I already knew what the argument was probably about. I continued eating my food, but Q decided to go check on his boy. Nicola came downstairs a few minutes later mean mugging me but I ignored the bitch eating my chicken because whatever just happened, she was handling it with the right person. There was no need for her to bring that shit down here

71

to me because I didn't bring her up here to the cabin just to play her.

"What?" I asked her because she just wouldn't stop staring.

"Don't say shit to me," she barked.

"I won't have to say anything to you if you stop fucking staring at me," I barked back.

"I know you bitches not tripping on Malik hoe ass when he not trying to wife you or you," Katrina laughed, pointing at the both of us.

I knew she had to be gone because she would never blow up my spot when she clearly sees Aaron sitting here, so I was going to let that slide.

"Trust me when I say that I don't want the nigga to wife me, but I be damned if he's going to be sneak fucking this bitch when he has me here with him," Nicola stressed and if looks could kill, I would be dead right now.

"What is she talking about?" Aaron asked.

Now I had two options on how I wanted to handle this and since I wasn't ready to answer Aaron's question, I focused on her ass.

Giving My Heart to A Gangsta

"I don't know what the fuck you're talking about, Nicola, so don't be trying to start no shit because that nigga Malik not giving you any attention," I snapped.

"So, you didn't just fuck that nigga?" She waited.

"Nah, that would make me a hoe and I only see one hoe in this room," I told her.

"Fuck you bitch!" She yelled.

"Call me a bitch again and see if I don't fuck you up." I dared her.

"Ugly bitch, fat bitch, nasty bitch and a thirsty fucking bitch," she spat, and I pounced on her ass.

"What the fuck are you two bitches doing?" I heard Katrina say before helping Aaron get me off that bitch.

Q and Malik walked back into the front room and this bitch started showing out thinking that Malik was going to protect her ass. I didn't even want to fight the bitch. I just didn't want to deal with Aaron feelings right now about what she said, but I knew that I was going to have to.

"Malik, why don't you tell Aaron that you just fucked this bitch like we weren't right downstairs with your disrespectful ass," she barked at him.

Londyn

"Why don't the fuck you stay in your lane and enjoy this free trip that your ass is on. Now go sit your ass down!" He yelled at her.

"I don't care if I'm on a free trip or not, I'm not going to be here and allow you to disrespect me like I'm nobody," she said, getting in her feelings.

"It's because your nobody to him, dumb ass. Now, go sit down like he said," I told her.

"I'm ready to go, Malik," she demanded.

"Well, you better get on your phone and see if Uber will come and get your ass because I'm not leaving until Sunday," he barked.

"Tamika, what the hell is going on between the two of you?" Aaron asked me.

"Yo, playboy, she doesn't have to explain shit to you. You not even getting the pussy," Malik said, taking the shit too far.

He must have hit a nerve because Aaron responded with his fist to Malik's mouth and they started fighting, breaking up shit in the process. I don't know if it was because Malik was high and drunk, but Aaron was tagging that ass and when Q jumped in, panic sunk in. Katrina sobered up quick and tried to

74

help me get them up off him. They weren't about to have us up in here witnessing a murder.

"Q, stop before you kill him," she tried pulling him off Aaron.

I had a new respect for Aaron even though I knew that after tonight he wasn't going to speak to me anymore. He wasn't going out like a punk because he was still fighting instead of covering up to avoid hits he was giving them back. After we finally got them from killing Aaron, he didn't even look at me and I felt bad. He got his things from the room and offered Nicola a ride back to the city which she accepted, leaving me feeling a way. I didn't say anything because I was wrong. I sat on the couch in my feelings because I really liked Aaron and I messed it up for a nigga that wouldn't even claim me the way Q claims Katrina.

"Are you ok?" Katrina asked me.

"No, but I'll be ok," I told her.

"Ok, I'm going to go check on Q and Malik," she said, leaving me to my thoughts.

Chapter Eight
(Tamika)

It's been about a week since everything went down in the Poconos and Aaron still wasn't speaking to me. I waited outside of his Chemistry class for him yesterday just for him to walk right by me like he never knew me. I even been calling and texting him to apologize just for him to ignore me like he didn't care about my apology. Malik, on the other hand, has been trying to see me but I was upset with him because all of this was his fault. I felt he took advantage of the situation because I was drinking and to repeat to Aaron what I said about my not sleeping with him was wrong on so many levels. I knew that Aaron goes by his grandmother's house every day after school, so I took my chances by going there. I knocked on the door and when she answered the door, she looked healthier than an ox, so I was confused. I thought she would be his ailing grandmother being he said that he came here every day to help her out before going home.

"Hello, young lady. How can I help you?" She asked me.

Giving My Heart to A Gangsta

"I'm sorry to bother you ma'am, but I'm a friend of Aaron and I came by to talk to him." I responded nervously.

"Well, come in and make yourself comfortable. He should be here soon," she offered, allowing me in which she shouldn't have, not knowing me.

I walked inside, took a seat on the couch and watched the television that she had on the TV One channel. I heard little feet running down the hallway and when I looked up, it was a little boy that looked to be about a year old.

"Hey, grandma baby. You up from your nap already?" She asked him, but he just smiled.

"We have company. What is your name young lady?" She asked.

"I'm Tamika, ma'am," I told her.

"Tamika, this is Aaron Jr," she said, causing my eyes to buck.

"Aaron didn't tell you that he had a son?" She questioned.

"No ma'am, he didn't."

"My daughter and Aaron dated for two years. When she got pregnant, I was upset but she was my baby, so I supported their decision to keep the baby. When she gave birth, she had complications due to her hemorrhaging and died after giving birth to him. Aaron and I made the decision for me to raise him while he finished school, but he's a big part of his life which I'm thankful for," she said proudly.

After hearing that, I felt like I was invading his personal life and I didn't want to be here right now. Just as I was going to leave, the knock came on the door. I knew that it was him and I was nervous as to how he was going to respond to me being here.

"Hey, Aaron. You have a visitor," I heard her say to him after opening the door.

As soon as he saw me, he mean-mugged me until his son ran to him and his face softened as he interacted with him. He spent almost an hour with his son without saying anything to me, but I stayed because I needed to talk to him. He kissed his son telling him that he would see him tomorrow, causing him to cry knowing his daddy was leaving.

"Ms. Green, I'm going to go but I will see you tomorrow," he said to her.

"Nice meeting you, Tamika and you be sure to treat Aaron right because he's a good man," she said to me, but I have no idea why when I told her that we were just friends.

Giving My Heart to A Gangsta

"Why the fuck would you come here, Tamika? And how the fuck did you even know which apartment?" He asked forgetting that he told me the apartment she lived in.

"I'm here because you're not trying to speak to me, so I figured if I showed up here you would have no choice. So, can you please just talk to me?" I pleaded.

"Tell me why I should talk to you after you played me?" He barked, causing me to jump back.

"Can we go somewhere and talk without you screaming at me like you're getting ready to hit me?" I asked him.

He didn't answer; he just walked to the elevator and I followed him until he reached his car. When he popped the locks, I got in. We didn't speak the entire ride to his house which I was thankful for because I didn't know what I wanted to say. Well, I knew what I needed to say but I didn't know how to word it so that he knows I'm truly sorry. His parents weren't home, so we ended up going to his bedroom to talk. I decided to just tell him the truth.

"Listen, Aaron. I never meant to disrespect you the way that I did and for that, I'm sorry. I should have told you that Malik and I have been sleeping together. To be honest, I didn't think that it would happen again until I let the liquor cloud my judgment when I saw how you were dancing with Nicola."

"So, you fucked someone in the same house that you knew that it would be a problem if I found out just because you saw me dancing? I came there with you, so I would never disrespect you in that way. I don't know what you thought you saw because it wasn't like I was up on her," he said making me think that I saw what I wanted to see to give me an excuse to go and fuck Malik's ass.

"Are you still fucking that nigga?"

"No. I'm not even speaking to him right now because I'm trying to be with you," I told him, being honest again.

"I thought you said that I wasn't your type?" He responded.

"You weren't my type until I got to know you," I admitted.

"Tamika, I'm not for the bullshit so if you're on some bullshit, just walk away and leave me alone. I have a son to raise and I don't have time to be beefing with niggas over no female," he said.

Giving My Heart to A Gangsta

"Why didn't you tell me that you had a son? And why did you say that it was your grandmother that lived there?" I asked him.

"I didn't tell you because, like I told you, I liked you and I didn't know how you were going to feel about me having a son. I didn't want you to find out about him the way that you did but I was going to tell you once you said that you were going to give us a chance as a couple. His mother is no longer in the picture because she passed away after giving birth to him and that's the reason he lives with her mother. My parents are too busy to care for a child as you should already know. Every time you come here, they're never home. Anyway, if you want to be with me, you're going to have to stop seeing Malik."

"I already told you that I'm not even talking to him right now, so you have nothing to worry about," I told him.

He ordered some take-out and we just chilled watching movies until it was time for him to take me home. I didn't want to leave but I have never stayed out overnight on a school night, so I wasn't even going to push my luck. I was feeling Aaron. I just hoped that I could stay away from Malik like I promised because I was still feeling his ass too. When I got home, I went into my room to call Katrina to tell her that me and Aaron made up, but she didn't answer the phone. She was with Q all the time whenever she wasn't at school, forgetting that she still has a best friend who misses her. Q got her mother a job at his uncle's company working as a receptionist, so her home life was much better now. She got rid of that freeloading boyfriend of hers and she finally gave Katrina a curfew. Yes, a curfew. She didn't care that she was eighteen but they both made a lot of progress. Her mother was having Christmas dinner at her house this year and they invited my mother and me. I couldn't wait because Katrina's mom could cook her ass off. My phone alerted me that I had a text message and it was Malik telling me that he was in the lobby of my building. I didn't want any problems between me and Aaron being we just started speaking again. I told him he could come up so that I could tell him to his face that it was over.

After I let him in, I took him to my room that he was all too familiar with so that we could talk, Also, so he could say what he needed to say.

"Malik, say whatever it is that you need to say so that you can go," I told him because I didn't want his ass getting comfortable.

I wanted to hear what he had to say before I told him that we could no longer sneak around sleeping together. I'd rather be somebody's girlfriend instead of somebody's booty call. I was done being his behind closed doors secret fuck buddy.

"I been trying to reach out to you to apologize for that shit that went down at the cabin. I was high and drunk, and in my feelings seeing you with that nigga after you just let me hit. I fucked up by treating you like you were a hoe. So, for that, I apologize and want us to start over," he said.

I wasn't expecting him to want to be with me so now my ass was conflicted being this is what I wanted from the jump. I wanted to be with Aaron, but I couldn't shake the feelings that I was having for Malik.

"So, you're not going to say anything?" He interrupted my thoughts.

I watched him, trying to study him to see if he was being real with me or just fucking with me. I don't know if he was saying all these things just because he didn't want me to be with Aaron or if he really wanted to be with me. I decided that if he was playing games, we were both going to play them together. I wasn't going to let Aaron go until he proved to me that he was serious about being with me.

"Malik, I swear you better not being trying to play me," I told him.

Londyn

"Only thing I'm trying to play with right now is that pussy," he smirked.

"Nope, your ass is on punishment," I laughed, kicking at his hands because he was trying to pull my pants down.

"Stop playing. I told you that I was sorry so get over here and let me show you how sorry I am," he laughed.

"Malik, you have to get ready to go. My mother is going to be home soon, so we will get up another time," I lied knowing my mother was doing a double tonight.

I just wanted us to chill and not have sex because of Aaron but his ass was being persistent, and it was hard turning him down knowing I wanted the dick. It wasn't like I was sleeping with two men at the same time being that Aaron and I haven't slept together. So, I convinced myself to give in and stop fighting the inevitable. He fucked me straight to sleep with a smile on my face.

Chapter Nine
(Katrina)

I was up early in the kitchen with my mother helping her start Christmas dinner because we were having guest over. I invited Q and he told me that my mother invited his uncle, so I been hinting around trying to figure out if her and his uncle was seeing each other. I had a feeling that if they weren't seeing each other, she was liking him because he's all that she talks about. She be like 'Q uncle Vick did this or he said that'; she was crushing on his ass. He was a nice-looking man that led me to believe that it ran in the family. If she was feeling him, I totally understood the how and why. Q never had a conversation with me about his parents or if he had any siblings. When I would ask, he would only reply that his uncle is his only family. My mom put the turkey in the oven while I started working on the sides as I sung to the Temptations Song *Silent Night* that my mom had playing. I was also thinking about my aunt peach cobbler that I couldn't wait to go in on.

After we finished cooking, my mom and I got washed and dressed before straightening up a little before the guest were to arrive. Tamika was the first one to arrive, saying that her mother was going to try and stop by when she got off work. She was telling me about how Malik told her that he wanted to be with her and how she was going to continue to see Aaron. I told her that it wasn't a smart move because someone could get hurt by her playing with a nigga feelings and shit, but she wasn't listening. She went on trying to justify her actions by saying that Malik could just be saying he wanted to be with her because he didn't want her with Aaron.

Then she said Aaron lied about him visiting his grandmother and that he was visiting his son that he had with some female, but she died after giving birth.

She was blowing my ear off. All I wanted to do was concentrate on getting my grub on and enjoy some family time with family I haven't seen in like forever. My grandmother Ella arrived from Virginia last night and she stayed at my aunt Laverne's house, so they will be coming together. Last year, I spent Christmas with my grandmother and made plans to visit again but never got the chance to, so I'm so excited right now to see her again. Q gave me some money, so I went to the Bath & Body Works store and got my mother, aunt, grandmother and Tamika all something. That five-dollar sell was the shit and carried my money a long way. I still walked out with cash in my bag. I was now sitting on the couch waiting and wishing that Q hurried up and got his ass here. Between Tamika and my aunt Laverne, they were getting on my nerves. My aunt keeps sweating me about going to college after I graduate high school, but I keep telling her ass that I had plans on going just not right out of high school.

"Laverne, leave that girl alone," my grandmother told her.

"Thank you, grandma," I said to her and smirked at my aunt.

Tamika was on her phone playing the dangerous game that has now become her life with her silly ass. I don't understand how she went from feeling a way about how Malik was treating her just to do the same thing to Aaron when he didn't deserve the shit. Q called my phone to let me know that him and his uncle was on their way up, so when I told my mother, she started setting the table. Yes, we weren't allowed to eat until her little crush got to the house so now we were about to get our grub on. I didn't care about the food right now because I just wanted to see my boo and I couldn't wait to give him his Christmas gift later tonight.

When Q walked through the door, he had this look on his face. I didn't know what it was about until I saw his uncle walk in with some bitch. The look on my mother's face made me want to go the fuck off because he had to know that she wasn't inviting him just because. She was feeling him so for him to show up with this female was disrespectful. I was ready to kick him the fuck out. I pulled Q to the side because I wanted to know why would he allow his uncle to walk up in here with another woman after we have had conversations about my mother feeling his uncle.

"Who the fuck is that bitch?" I asked him once we were in the privacy of my room.

"That's his wife!" he blurted out.

"His wife? So, when I told you that I think that my mother was feeling your uncle, why you never mentioned he had a wife? And why is she here with him? Better yet, why the fuck did he show up knowing he had a wife?" I shot off question after question because I was tight right now.

"Look, it's one of those situations to where him and his wife aren't on good terms but still husband and wife. So, when he told her that he was invited to Christmas dinner, she wanted to know who would invite him and not invite his wife. He tried to back out of coming but then she started accusing him of shit so to shut her up, he told her that she could come with him," he tried to justify his uncle's actions.

I was now ready to kick him out, his uncle and that ugly ass wife of his; he just pissed me off. I walked back into the living room and asked my mother if I could speak to her for a second. If she was uncomfortable about the situation, I was kicking them the fuck out.

"Mom, if you want, I will have them leave," I said to her.

"It's fine, honey. I knew that he had a wife, but he told me that they weren't on good terms; that's why I invited him. I had no idea that he was going to show up with his wife. Another reason I extended the invite was because he said that he was going to be spending Christmas alone. I was shocked to see him walk through the door with her, but we're not going to let it ruin Christmas dinner," she said with a smile on her face, but I knew that she was bothered.

We walked back out to Aunt Laverne fixing plates, so we decided to help her. Even though I was still pissed at Q, I fixed his plate.

"Who made the macaroni and cheese?" Vick's wife asked.

"I made it, why?" My aunt asked, automatically getting defensive.

Londyn

"I just asked because I've never known anyone to use white cheddar mixed with sharp cheddar," she responded.

"First off, I didn't put any white cheddar in the macaroni; it's mozzarella. And before you ask why I use mozzarella... I use it because it's my recipe and not yours," my aunt barked because she was very sensitive about her food.

"I wasn't trying to offend you, I was just asking. There was no need to get all bent out of shape about it," she responded.

"I'm telling you, ya'll better get her because she doesn't know me," my aunt said before going into the kitchen slamming shit and mumbling to herself.

She was trying to calm herself down and I was trying not to laugh because anyone who comes to any dinners we have never eats aunt Laverne mac and cheese. She says it's mozzarella, but it always looked like mayonnaise to everyone else, so we always passed. My mother knew this, so I know why his wife was the only one with aunt Laverne's mac and cheese. Her own mama never ate her mac and cheese and we always switched it out with my mother's mac and cheese. My uncle Fizz thought the shit was so funny that he couldn't stop laughing until my granny told him to shut the hell up. They

Giving My Heart to A Gangsta

knew if aunt Laverne started up, there was no way in hell we would get her to stop until she beat somebody ass. When all was calm again, we enjoyed dinner with normal conversation. I was getting a bit nervous that something was going to jump off because Q's uncle was in here low-key flirting with my mother. I was praying that my mother wasn't about to play the position of his side chick because her ass was giggling like a damn love-struck teenager.

After dinner, we sat around listening to Christmas music while we enjoyed my aunt's peach cobbler; the one thing that she could make well. Someone knocked at the door, so I got up to answer it. It was Malik and he didn't look like himself. He asked for Q and they spoke in hush tones until Q apologized but said that he had to take care of something. I was upset because it was Christmas, so I felt whatever business he needed to tend to could have waited. No longer than five minutes later, we heard gunshots ring out. I ran for the door because Q and Malik had just left, but my mom pulled me back. His uncle told us to stay put while him and my uncle Fizz went to see what was going on. I was so scared because I knew that he was in the streets. Add to the fact that they had beef with some dudes in my building. Uncle Fizz came back. He said that it was a bad scene and we needed to stay in the apartment.

Londyn

"Uncle Fizz, did you see Q or Malik?" I asked him.

"It's a bad scene baby girl," he responded, pissing me off.

"What the fuck does that mean? Did you see Q or Malik?" I questioned again and when he wouldn't make eye contact, I ran out of the apartment with Tamika right behind me.

I heard my mother screaming my name, but I kept going because I needed to make sure that Q and Malik were ok. I took the back stairwell to the floor that Tierra lived on because that's the floor that they were on handling business last time. Tamika caught up to me and told me to just wait because it was police everywhere, but I couldn't wait. I needed to know if they were hurt or not. As soon as I opened the door, I saw a few bodies laid out in the hallway and the tears flooded my face, blurring my vision. I saw Q's uncle on his knees and I just knew that it was Q, but when I got a closer look, I saw that it was Malik. Tamika and I tried to get to him, but the police weren't allowing anyone pass where we were now standing. I was in panic mode not knowing if Q was one of the dudes lying on the floor with gunshot wounds. EMS arrived on the scene and that's when they cleared the hallway. So I went downstairs to the first floor outside with all the other onlookers. Q wasn't one of the guys that were hurt so I was confused as to where he was and why would he leave Malik.

Giving My Heart to A Gangsta

Tamika was crying, and I tried my best to console her, but I was worried about Q whereabouts. We were all downstairs trying to get answers as to what happened but when the police started questioning people, Q's uncle pulled us back inside. Tamika cried about wanting to ride with Malik to the hospital, but he told her that it would be best for now that we just go inside. I asked him if he knew where Q was, and he said that he didn't know. Malik was unresponsive, so he said that we all needed to pray for him.

I wasn't trying to hear him. I needed to know if Q was ok. He could have been somewhere bleeding out and he wanted us to do nothing. Somebody needed to be at the hospital for Malik being we didn't know who to call for him. Right now, we were all he had.

"Mom, I think that we should go to the hospital to see about Malik until someone contacts his family," I said to her with tears falling from my eyes.

"I handled it," Q's uncle Vick said. He was about to get cursed out because he was acting fucking secretive and now wasn't the time.

Chapter Ten
(Katrina)

I was blowing up Q's phone trying to get in touch with him because I was seconds away from going off on his fucking uncle. I don't even know why he and his fucking wife were still here anyway when they should have left already. I looked out my window and my block looked like a damn warzone right now with all these damn police cars and the entire hood being outside.

"Did you get in touch with him yet?" Tamika asked me.

"He's not answering and I'm starting to worry that he might be somewhere bleeding out," I told her trying to fight back tears.

"I hope not but I think that we need to go to the hospital to see about Malik. Fuck what Q uncle is talking about," she said, and I agreed with her.

We walked to Delancey Street and hailed a cab to Beth Israel hospital, praying that they took him there being it was the closest. When we got there, I went to the front pretending to be his sister once Tamika gave me his last name. I don't

94

think she believed me, but she told me that he was there, but he was in surgery. She added that someone would be out to talk to his family as soon as they had an update, so we went to sit in the waiting area. I tried Q again just to get his voicemail, so I left a message this time telling him to contact me as soon as he gets my message.

We were now at the hospital for about an hour before Q walked in with like ten niggas wearing all black. He looked like he was ready to be on some murder one shit, so I second guessed my wanting to jump in his arms. The scowl on his face was vicious and just when I thought he was walking towards me, him and his entourage walked right passed me. He walked over to some dudes that I didn't pay much attention to until now and noticed that it was Raheem who stayed in my building. Raheem was sitting over there with his crew and nervousness started to sink in because I just knew it was about to be some shit. When Raheem stood, his crew followed suit. I got scared as shit because I didn't know who was strapped and who wasn't. Even the security guard looked like he was about to shit on himself, so I knew he wouldn't be able to do shit if something popped off.

"Who the fuck was those niggas?" Q barked, getting in Raheem's face.

Londyn

"Yo, Q, I don't know who the fuck those niggas were. My nigga laid up in this bitch just like Malik," Raheem barked back.

"So, these niggas just walk up busting guns, and nobody knows who the fuck they are?" Q questioned. I just knew that the security guard was going to intervene, but he wasn't saying shit.

"That's what the fuck I'm saying. We been doing business for how long? We never had any problems, so why start now? My nigga fighting for his life and two didn't make it, so I'm just as pissed as you are," he told Q.

"Well, whoever those niggas were better hope I don't find out because every one of them are going to wish their mothers swallowed," he barked before walking away like a boss.

"You good?" He asked, giving me a hug.

"You had me thinking that something happened to you by ignoring my calls," I cried, pulling away from him.

"I'm sorry, shorty. Trust if I could have answered, I would have. Did they give an update on Malik?" He asked.

"No, all we know is that he's still in surgery," I told him.

Giving My Heart to A Gangsta

"Yo, keep me posted because it's about to be hot up here, so I'm out," he said and just like that, he was gone.

"I don't know if I'm cut out to deal with this shit, Tamika. I think after we find out that Malik is good, I'm walking away from Q. Who's to say that I'm not with him when niggas decide to roll up on his ass or he decides to roll up on their ass. I think you should be done with Malik and stick with Aaron because if we stay with them, we're going to need bullet proof vests," I laughed nervously but I was dead serious.

I'm eighteen years young and I'm trying to live to see eighteen more so it's for the best that I leave his ass alone.

"I feel you, Katrina, but I don't know if I can just walk away," she said, sounding stupid as shit.

It might be easier for me being I didn't get a taste of Q's dick yet, so I'm not dickmitized. Malik got her ass playing Aaron so she's dickmitized already if after this scene tonight wasn't enough for her to walk away. To be honest, I was ready to leave the hospital and take my ass home because this bad vibe I was feeling was something serious. My mom was blowing up my phone because it was getting late, so I knew she wanted me to be walking through her door.

Londyn

"Tamika, I have to go because my mom is blowing up my phone, but I don't want to leave you." I told her.

"You can go, I'll be ok," she said. The way she said it let me know that she was going to be upset if I left.

Just as I was about to respond to her, a woman and an older gentleman walked up to the window inquiring about Malik. She told the man behind the glass that she was his mother and the gentleman was his grandfather. A few seconds later, a female carrying a kid came in crying and upset, asking his mother what were they saying. I wasn't trying to ear hustle, but I wanted to know who she was to Malik but had an idea.

"I don't know what MJ and I are going to do if something happens to Malik," she cried, and his mother tried comforting her.

"I'm ready," Tamika said as she stood and rolled her eyes at the family before walking out.

"All this fucking time I thought he was hiding me because of my age, but this motherfucker has a bitch and a fucking son," she vented as I flagged a cab, just happy to be going home.

"Fuck those niggas, Q knew his ass was playing me," she spat.

Giving My Heart to A Gangsta

"It wasn't Q's place to tell you that man's business. The only nigga that owed you the truth was Malik," I told her, defending his ass after I just said that I was done with him.

"Well, Q ass probably playing your ass too," she huffed but I let her have it because I wasn't about to go there with her.

She was upset about Malik lying to her, but she was lying to him too. It was a fair exchange, no robbery, so she needed to get over it. She didn't have to be mad at Q because I knew that she was seeing Aaron. If I told Q and he told Malik, she would be upset with me. Malik is his friend, so I doubt that he would have ratted his friend out the same way I wouldn't rat her ass out. I paid the cab when we pulled up to my building and she said that she would see me tomorrow before walking way with her stank attitude.

After filling my mother in on what happened at the hospital, which wasn't much, I went to shower so that I could get into bed. I was tired and just wanted to go to sleep because Christmas and my plan to seduce Q was a flop. Well, it saved me from giving myself to someone I didn't plan on being with, so I guess it played out in my favor. I called Tamika before going to bed to make sure that she was good, but the call went to voicemail, letting me know that she's in her feelings.

Londyn

I heard my phone ringing after I just put it on the charger, so I got out of bed thinking it was Tamika calling to apologize for her stink ass not answering, but it was Q.

"Hello," I yawned into the phone, pretending that he woke me up.

"Hey, was you sleeping?" He asked me.

"Yeah, but what's up?" I asked him.

"I'm just calling to let you know that Malik is out of surgery and expected to make a full recovery, so let your girl know."

"I'm sure that his girl and son will be happy," I responded, being sarcastic.

"Look shorty, that's not our business. That's between Malik and your girl," he barked.

"I'm tired, Q, so I'm going to call you tomorrow," I told him, ending the call.

I wasn't about to sit on the phone with him telling me what was my business when it came to my best friend. I agree with him that it was Malik's business to tell her, but his ass had me fucked up if he thought I wasn't going to ride with my girl on this. I tried Tamika's phone again, but she sent the call to voicemail again. I decided not to sweat it and take my ass to sleep for school tomorrow.

Walking out of the building the next morning, I rolled my eyes in the back of my head seeing Q parked and waiting on me. I knew that I needed to tell him that I couldn't see him anymore because whatever we had going on wasn't enough to risk my life.

"Q, I didn't need for you to come pick me up," I told him with agitation in my voice.

"What's wrong with you?" He barked.

"Nothing is wrong with me. I just didn't need for you to come pick me up," I spat.

"I didn't ask you if you needed me to pick you up because you didn't have a problem with all the other times I picked your ass up."

"Listen, I'm just going to tell you the truth, Q. I'm not cut out for this street life that you got going on and I want no parts of it. I'm not trying to get my life cut short just because I'm feeling you, so I think it's best that we don't see each other anymore."

Londyn

"So, you think that I would let something happen to you when I been protecting your ass since the fucking day I started kicking it with you?" He growled.

"I'm not saying that you would let it happen intentionally, but you have beef in these streets and I just don't want to get caught in the middle of the shit."

"So, you going to sit here and judge me, acting like you didn't know I was a hood nigga when you used to watch me like some crazed stalker," he chuckled.

He was right. I did know that he was a hood nigga, but I didn't know that my life would be at risk being in his presence. It was going to be hard letting him go because I was feeling his ass that much. But, I had to do what I had to do.

"Q, I'm not trying to judge you. I'm just trying to keep it real with you about how I'm feeling, I just need you to respect it," I told him.

"I wouldn't be real if I respected that bullshit you spitting, Katrina. You live in the fucking projects, so you risk getting caught up in some shit every day," he barked, hurting my feelings just a bit.

Giving My Heart to A Gangsta

"I live in the projects, but I don't have a choice. I do have a choice when it comes to risking my life by being with you Q!" I shouted.

"So, how about I move you up out of these projects, Katrina? You and your mother." he said, causing me to look at him like he's crazy.

"How are you going to move me and my mother up out of the projects, Q?" I asked in disbelief.

"Listen, I'm feeling you and I willing to do whatever I need to do to make you feel safe. You don't have to answer me now, Katrina. I'm going to drop you off at school and come by and talk to you and your mother later," he said with a straight face.

I told him that I wasn't making any promises about seeing him later but allowed him to take me to school because if I got out, I was going to be late. When I got to school, I noticed that Tamika wasn't in class, but I chalked it up to maybe her being late, but she never showed. I tried calling her on my lunch break, but she didn't answer the call and I was started to feel a way about her taking her attitude out on me. I didn't fuck her and not tell her about a relationship and kid, so she needed to save that shit for Malik's ass. After school, Q was waiting and I

Londyn

swear I was hoping that he didn't show up to pick me up because I needed to go see about Tamika. He said that he needed to make a stop when I got in the car, so I just laid my head back saying nothing.

Chapter Eleven
(Katrina)

When Q said he had a stop to make, I had an idea that he was going to the hospital and I was in utter shock to see Tamika's ass in the room chilling with Malik. Last conversation we had, she said fuck both those niggas, so I guess it was just fuck me. I was in my feelings right now and she needed to explain how she was curbing my calls but sitting up here laughing with the nigga that lied to her ass.

"Tamika, let me speak to you," I said, pulling her ass out into the hallway not waiting on her to answer.

"Girl, stop pulling on me. What the hell is your problem?" She asked dumbly.

"So, you up here entertaining this nigga but ignoring my calls. What happened to fuck him?" I barked.

"Katrina, calm your dramatic ass down acting like we're not in a hospital full of sick people with your crazy ass," she laughed.

Londyn

"I'm not laughing, Tamika. You treat me like I did something to you when he was the one that lied to you. He gets a visit and I get sent to voicemail," I stressed.

"I'm sorry, Katrina. I was going to call you as soon as I left the hospital," she said with her lying ass.

"So, you forgave him for lying to you?" I asked her.

"He didn't lie. He just didn't get around to telling me," she said, sounding stupid.

"Tamika, please tell me you're joking right now. He didn't get around to telling you about having a girl and a son? Yeah, ok."

"She's not his girl, just the mother of his son."

"Anyway, I told Q that I didn't think I could see him anymore, but he wasn't trying to hear me. He even offered to move me and my mother out of the projects," I told her, changing the subject.

"He what? Damn, I knew those niggas had bank. So, are you trying to move and what did your mother say?" She asked, getting all excited.

"I didn't tell my mother and he only offered because I told him that I didn't want to see his ass anymore. They have beef

106

in these streets and we can become a target at any time," I stressed to her.

"Well, at least he's trying to put you and your mom in a better environment. Did he say what neighborhood he was trying to move you to?"

"Nope and I didn't ask him because I knew it was just a ploy for me to stay with his ass."

"Well, it must have worked because you just showed up with him and to be honest, I don't think that you should end things with him. Especially based on his dealings in the streets because we live in the hood and at any given time, we could have gotten caught in the line of fire," she said, sounding like Q's ass.

"I have to think about it, Tamika. This shit scares me," I said, being honest.

"It scares me too. I just knew that Malik was going to die and that's something that I wasn't ready to endure," She responded.

We went back into the hospital room and I expressed to Malik how I was happy that he was feeling better before taking a seat next to Q.

Londyn

"Listen, I was just talking to Malik and he agrees that since the two of you are fucking with us, it's best that you both get out of the projects. My uncle just finished a two-family house in a nice area of Queens. Before you say anything, Katrina, just know that I'm not taking no for an answer. Speak to your moms and let them know what's up," he demanded.

"I speak for myself and my mom when I say hell yeah!" Tamika screeched, dancing in her seat.

"Well, I don't speak for my mother, so I'll have to let you know," I told him, causing him to take a deep breath.

I'm sorry that I didn't share the same reaction as Tamika, but it is what it is, and I didn't care how they felt. He wasn't going to force me to decide to leave where I called home in a matter of seconds. I had to be the voice of reason. What happens if we break up? Does that mean that we would have to leave after giving up our apartment? We couldn't afford to live in New York without living in the projects, so yes, there were things to think about and shit to discuss. He would have to put all that paperwork in my mama's name because she didn't raise no fool just like her mama didn't raise no fool. If Q was cool with doing that then I'd be the first to tell Gompers Housing Project to kiss my ass because I was moving on to bigger and better.

Giving My Heart to A Gangsta

"What you over there smiling about?" Q smirked.

I didn't even realize that I was smiling but it would feel good to finally get out of the projects and the drama that came with living in them. My mother has been down to housing court just about every other month to avoid getting evicted, and in return, having to go down to the welfare office for a one-shot deal.

"I wasn't smiling but I will talk to my mother. What I do know is that she's not going to want to move until I finish school. The commute from Queens every day is going to be crazy," I told him.

We left the hospital and he dropped me off at home so that I could talk to my mother. I knew she wasn't home yet, so I checked the mail before getting on the elevator. Just the thought of not having to live under these conditions anymore caused a wide smile to spread across my face. My mom came home about an hour later walking through the door singing. She didn't even notice me sitting on the couch as she continued to sing and dance. I watched as she sat her bag down on the counter and removed her jacket, still getting her dance on, causing me to smile.

"Somebody is happy," I said, startling her.

"Katrina, you scared me," she laughed as she grabbed her chest.

"What got you in such a good mood?" I asked her.

"Life baby girl, life," she sang.

"I need to talk to you about something?" I said to her seriously.

"Katrina, please don't ruin my day by telling me you're pregnant," she said just as serious.

"Mom, you have to be having sex to get pregnant," I sighed.

"Thank you, Jesus, because I was just about to have a heart attack," she laughed. "Now what is it that you need to talk to me about?"

"Well, the incident that happened on Christmas with Q and Malik scared me, so I told Q that I didn't feel safe and couldn't see him anymore. He suggested moving us out of the projects so that I could feel safe being that it happened in our building. He said that his uncle just completed a two-family home in Queens that me, you, Tamika and her mother could live in," I informed her, and it still sounded crazy to me.

Giving My Heart to A Gangsta

"I hope his ass don't think that I'm going to give up my apartment to live somewhere that he could kick us out of whenever the hell he gets ready. If he's being generous then he needs to be generous and say he's going to put all the paperwork in my name before I even consider it," she responded the way I thought she would.

"I was thinking the same thing, but Tamika told him that she made the decision for her mom and that she accepts," I told her, shaking my head.

"Tamika thinks she can make decisions for her mom, but I know her mom and she's going to be saying the same shit I just said," she said, getting up to go to the kitchen.

Her phone rang, and she excused herself to take the call. I knew that it was Q's uncle and I prayed she wasn't trying to get caught up with a married man. Her choice of men always sucked. Now that she got rid of her bum ass boyfriend, I don't want her getting caught up with a man that doesn't belong to her. I don't care how many times he says he's having issues in his relationship, I wasn't buying it. If he was having problems, there's no way she would have convinced him to bring her with him anywhere if he didn't want her there. The only problem his ass probably was having in his relationship was the fact that he didn't want to be a one-woman man anymore.

Londyn

After dinner, I was on FaceTime with Q until my eyes were trying to close. So before ending the call, I told him that he could come by tomorrow to speak to my mother. My grandmother was leaving on Sunday, so we were visiting her at my auntie house to have dinner since Christmas dinner got interrupted with the hood drama. I already knew that I was going to have to hear how she didn't approve of Q after she found out that he was involved in the bloodbath that took place in my building. Q had the nerve to ask if I wanted him to go with me and I had to tell him hell no. The grandmother he encountered was the nice version of her. The grandmother that I was going to see on Saturday is the one that was going to get in me and my mother's ass on some no holds barred type shit.

I woke up the next morning feeling like I never went to sleep last night. I was still tired as I dragged my feet. I swear, if I didn't have a final today, I would have stayed my ass home in bed since my mother was already gone. She had to take two buses to get to work so she leaves at six every morning. But like I said, I had a final which meant I had to take my ass to school. Q let me know that he wasn't going to be able to take me to school or pick me up, so I was catching a ride with Tamika and Aaron this morning. Yes, her ass was still creeping with this nigga but who was I to judge? I just kept my feelings to myself since she didn't take heed to my earlier advice about her situation.

After taking my final, I felt like I aced it, so I was feeling good sitting at a table in the cafeteria. That was until Tierra ass sat down. She knew that we didn't fuck with each other so why she decided to sit at my table when she had so many choices was mind boggling to me. I wasn't about to entertain her ass, so I grabbed my tray to move to another table.

"Katrina, wait. I'm not here to start any trouble. I just want to talk to you," she said, stopping me.

"Talk to me about what?" I asked with raised eyebrows.

"I just want to apologize to you for everything that I put you through behind that no-good man of mines. I was just jealous that he was always checking for you," she admitted.

"I never understood why you kept coming for me when you always saw that I never paid his ass any attention. I would never do anything like that to you, let alone any female for that matter," I told her.

"I know and again, I'm sorry and hope that you let me make it up to you to show you no more hard feelings. Do you think that you could hang out afterschool for about an hour to go to the mall?" She asked me.

Londyn

I told her that I could hang with her for about an hour since Tamika was hanging out with Aaron afterschool and Q wasn't coming over until seven. Once school ended, I waited in front of the building with her and she told me that she had to make a stop before we headed to the mall. I didn't see a problem with it since she said it was on the way to the mall. So, I agreed to go with her to wherever she had to make the stop. We got off the bus about a few blocks from Manhattan mall on the Westside before entering a complex. We took the elevator to the third floor and I just figured that it was a family apartment being she just walked in. When I walked in behind her, my eyes bulged, and my mouth was wide open as she stood there with a smirk on her face. I couldn't believe that Q was sitting on the couch letting that bitch Jemima suck his dick without a care in the world as he moaned, grabbing her head. So, I guess when he said he would handle it, this was his way of handling it; by continuing to fuck her so that she wouldn't say shit else to me.

I couldn't believe that I trusted that bitch Tierra just for her to play me. As much as I wanted to fuck her up, I just left. I could hear Q calling my name, but I ignored him as I found the stairwell and ran down the steps until I reached the front. I walked the few blocks until I made it to the mall, going into the bathroom and letting the tears fall, not believing that he would do some shit like that to me.

Chapter Twelve
(Quentin)

"So, you really trying to run behind that bitch?" Jemima barked.

I ran out of her apartment in just my damn boxers, not realizing I had no fucking clothes on until I reached the first floor and the air hit my ass.

"Jemima, you better shut up before I punch you dead in your shit for this petty bullshit you just pulled. I don't give a fuck how many times I stick my dick in your mouth, you will never be the bitch I chase. So yes, I'm about to chase the bitch that I want to be with so go suck on that, you miserable bitch. You and Tierra got me fucked up, but I could show you better than I could tell you," I barked.

"Q, I'm not scared of you and I didn't ask you to come here acting all thirsty to get your dick wet, so miss me with the threats. You should have been chasing her to ask her to get your dick wet, but we all know she not giving up the pussy, so I know you'll be back. Just so you know, when you come back, I'm going to give you the same treatment you're giving me now., she lied with a straight face, knowing she lived to get on her knees.

I didn't have time to stand there and argue with her ass, so I dashed up out of there to catch up with Katrina. I drove to the bus stop that she would have needed to get home, but she wasn't there, so I circled the block and a few other blocks before heading to her crib. I needed to explain to her that the shit she just witnessed didn't mean shit to me and she didn't need to be sweating it. When I got to her apartment, nobody answered the door, so I went back downstairs to my car and decided to wait on her, but she never showed. Her mom got to the building before her and being I was supposed to meet with her today, I got out of my car to greet her. I was hoping when we got inside that Katrina was going to be there and just didn't answer because she knew that it was me. Her mother called out to her, but she didn't answer so she went to her room to check; she wasn't there.

"Q, did you speak to Katrina?" She asked.

"I spoke to her earlier," I told her.

"It's late so she should have been home by now. Give me a second so that I can call Tamika to see if they are together," she stressed.

Londyn

She was starting to go into panic mode, so I knew that I had to say something before she called the police. She was pacing back and forth like she was about to lose her mind as Tamika's phone kept going to voicemail. After she tried to reach Katrina on her phone and it kept going to voicemail, I knew that I hesitated long enough and needed to tell her what was going on.

"I think I know why she's not answering the phone," I said to her.

"Well, are you going tell me?" She asked sarcastically.

"She showed up to a friend house that I was with today and she was with Tierra, but I don't know why she was with her. She saw me in a position that she shouldn't have, and she ran out of the building. I went after her, but she was gone by the time I got downstairs. I circled the blocks to no avail before coming here to wait on her."

"So, my daughter walked in on you having sex? And what the hell was she doing with Tierra?" She snapped.

"No, I wasn't having sex and I have no idea why she was with Tierra, but I do know that Tierra set her up to see me in that position."

Giving My Heart to A Gangsta

"Listen, I can't even deal with all of that right now. I need to find my daughter," she said just as Katrina walked through the door.

"Katrina, honey, are you alright?" She asked, hugging her.

"I'm fine but why is he here? He needs to leave." She rolled her eyes at me.

"Katrina, let me explain," I begged not sure how I was going to explain my dick being down another female's throat.

"Q, I'm not trying to hear nothing you have to say so you could do me a favor and let yourself out," she said, walking away, leaving me feeling defeated.

I decided that I was going to give her some time to get over the initial blow and hope that she would be willing to talk to me in a few days. I let her mother know that I still wanted to move them to the house that my uncle finished if that was something that they were still interested in, but she said she needed to tend to her daughter.

I ended up going to my uncle's house because I needed to talk to someone since Malik was still laid up in the hospital. I could have talked to my boys, but they would have been clowning my ass being I was in my feelings about losing

Katrina. I don't know what it was about her, but it was going to fuck me up if I lost her before officially having her.

"Hey unc," I said, giving him a dap.

"What do I owe this visit?" He chuckled.

He knows that the only time I visit him at his home is when I need to talk to him about something or need advice. I already spoke to him about the property, so he knew it was either some hood shit or a female.

"I messed up, unc and I don't know how to fix the shit. Katrina caught me with my pants down because the trick I was with set me up," I stressed.

"I'm going to be honest with you, nephew. Even if she forgives you, whatever she saw is going to be embedded into her head. You just gave her trust issues and an invitation to insecurities in the relationship if she decides to give you one. I say cut your losses on this one, move the hell on and save yourself from the headaches that's sure to come," he advised.

"So, that's your advice? Last I checked, you didn't want to be with your wife because of that same reason, but you stayed," I reminded him.

Giving My Heart to A Gangsta

"I stayed longer than I should have and wasted time on her when I could have been with someone else. So, when I speak, I speak from experience," he said.

I usually respect his advice, but this time, I wasn't feeling it. I messed up and needed to make it right. I trust that if she forgave me, she wouldn't hold it against me. I wasn't sleeping with her and someone else too.

"Let me find out that young girl got your ass open," he laughed.

"Same as her mother got your ass," I clapped back.

"So, what's up with those niggas that popped Malik?" He questioned, changing the subject.

I already knew he was creeping with Katrina's mom. I smelt his cologne all over her today with his sneaky ass.

"We still trying to find out who those niggas were with no such luck. Somebody has to know something. On my mother, I'm going to find those niggas and bury all their asses," I barked.

"I'm a retired gun but if you need your unc, you know I'll come out of retirement," he said, busting his fake gun with his hand, causing me to laugh.

Londyn

"Unc, trust me when I say I got this. What I don't got is any advice about how to get my girl back," I stressed.

"Spend some of that damn money you're sitting on, nigga, and be creative," he responded.

"I just spent ends buying that property that you just completed in Queens," I reminded him.

"Nah, do some personal shit to prove to her how much she means to you. Females live for that mushy shit. So, like I said, get those creative juices flowing and get your girl like I got her mama."

"Yeah, ok. Don't say shit when that wife of yours go upside your damn head because you know her ass is low-key crazy," I laughed.

I left his house with thoughts of what I was going to do to get her back, but I was drawing a blank and getting a damn headache. I called her phone just to see if she would take my call, but she let the call go to voicemail pissing me off. I decided to just send her a text to see if she would respond so I could try to get her to agree to go out with me. If she says that she will go out with me, I had no plans on what I was going to do because my creative juices were not flowing.

Giving My Heart to A Gangsta

Me- I know that you don't want to talk to me but I'm begging you to just give me a chance to take you out and explain.

I waited for her to respond. After like five minutes, I didn't think that she was going to respond, but I finally got the alert.

Katrina- Q, what could you possibly say to explain that bitch on her knees with your dick in her mouth? The same bitch that you told me that you weren't fucking with anymore. The same bitch that you said that you were going to handle. So, again, what could you possibly explain to me?

Me- Listen, before you strike me out, could you at least give me a chance to talk to you and apologize? I promise, if you never want to see me again after meeting with me, I'll leave you alone for good.

I told her that but if she shot me down, I wasn't going to leave her ass alone until she said that she forgave me, and we could start over.

Katrina- I'm going to my aunt house to see my grandmother on Saturday before she leaves to go back home. I can meet with you after I get home if it's not too late.

Me- Thank you. Just call me when you get home from her house and I'll come scoop you up.

Londyn

Katrina- Yeah, ok.

So, the easy part was over and that was getting her to agree to meet up with me. I had no idea what I was going to do to prove to her that I wanted to be with her and only her. I had a day and a half to come up with something. When I got home, I showered before getting in the bed. My phone alerted me of a text message and when I saw that it was Jemima, I knew that she wasn't going to just walk away. She was going to make sure to continue to cause problems with whoever I decided that I wanted to be with. She was delusional thinking that we had more than a sexual relationship going on, but I'm pulling the plug on sexing her ass too. If she wanted to continue getting this dick, she should have kept her fucking mouth closed and kept Katrina out of it. Even if I wasn't trying to be with Katrina, she would never be my girl. I don't know how many times I need to stress the same shit to her. If she doesn't know, she will soon enough.

Chapter Thirteen
(Tamika)

I had Aaron drop me off at Katrina's building. She called telling me that she hated Q and how she wished he got hit by a car. I tried getting her to tell me what the hell happened over the phone, but she started crying so I cut my date short to come see about her. It was late when I got to her house, so I called my mom to let her know that I was staying the night which she didn't have a problem with. After her mom let me in, I walked to her room and she was sitting on the bed Indian style watching tv. Her eyes were red from crying, so I needed her to tell me what Q did to her to have her in this state.

"So, what's going on?" I asked her.

"Yesterday in the cafeteria, Tierra sat down at my table and apologized for everything that happened between us. She invited me to go to the mall with her and I told her ok since you were going out with Aaron afterschool. Anyway, she tells me that she needed to make a stop about three blocks from the mall, so I didn't think anything of it. We get to the apartment building on the Westside and she opens the apartment door. As

125

soon as the door opened, I saw Q. He was sitting on the couch with Jemima on her knees and his dick in her mouth," she cried.

"So, the bitch set you up and you walked right into that shit, knowing by now that you can't trust her ass. I swear, I'm so sick of her fucking with you like you slept with that bum ass nigga that she's claiming. Now, as far as Q's ass, that shit was foul. He knows that you just had to fight that bitch. So, now he got you out here looking stupid. What are you going to do?" I wanted and needed to know if that meant we weren't moving anymore.

"He's supposed to be taking me out after I get home from my aunt's house on Saturday from seeing my grandmother. To be honest, I don't even want to fuck with him anymore. He has two strikes already, so I don't know if I want to wait around for the third," she stressed.

"Well, I have to keep it real with you, Katrina. We both know you wasn't giving the nigga any pussy. At the end of the day, he's a man and it wasn't like you caught him having sex with her up in that bitch. They love playing the game so my advice to you is to play the game too. Let his ass move you up out of here and hit him in his pockets. Fuck love," I told her.

Giving My Heart to A Gangsta

"Tamika, that's not me to just bluntly play someone. I treat people the way I want to be treated," she responded.

"So, how is that working for you? You better change that shit to treating people how they treat you because your way isn't working," I laughed.

"I hear what you're saying, but if I give him another chance, I'm not going to do him dirty or use him for his money. I think my giving him another chance has to do with Jemima doing all of this so that I could kick him to the curb. I want to show her that she could keep degrading herself and she's still not going to get his ass. All she's good for is getting a nigga dick wet."

"Yeah, but that's not going to hurt her. At the end of the day, she's still getting the dick that belongs to you. So, either you're going to put out or he's going to keep going to her ass to get his dick wet."

"I guess, but I'm not giving it up until I'm ready. I thought I was ready to give it to him, but he fucked that up. He has to work for it and if he's not willing to wait for it without messing with the next willing participant, then he'll just earn his third strike."

Londyn

She wasn't listening to me because he's not going to care to wait. His ass is going to be hitting everything moving. He's just going to be more careful while doing it next time, so she could hold out all she wants. I know one thing, I'm not trying to sit back and let her mess up my chances of getting up out of these damn projects.

I left Katrina's house early the next morning. After getting washed and dressed, I headed out to the hospital to visit Malik. I didn't get to see him yesterday, so I know he probably thinks that I'm upset about his son's mother showing up on my last visit, but that wasn't the reason. Aaron has become my addiction since blessing me with some bomb dick. I was craving him something terrible yesterday and that's why I didn't make it to the hospital.

Walking into his hospital room, my smile faded seeing that his son's mother was visiting again. The shit was starting to piss me off. I get that he has a son with her, but I'm sure her ass visiting so much has nothing to do with his son. I took a deep breath before walking over to the bed and kissing him on his lips, not giving a shit that she was sitting there. I heard her suck her teeth, but I didn't give a shit how she felt about me just like I didn't give a shit how his family felt either. He said his parents didn't care for me because they wanted him to be with her, so he doubt if they would like any female that wasn't her.

"You don't have to mark your territory with your desperate attempt of intimacy unless you're intimidated by me and it makes you feel better," she said.

"Kashari, don't start," Malik growled.

"Yes, Kashari, please don't start and get your ass kicked in front of your son," I told her.

"Watch your mouth in front of my son," she spat.

"I wouldn't have to watch my mouth in front of your son if you didn't come for me because I kissed my man. It shouldn't have bothered you unless you still want him," I accused.

"Little girl, if I still wanted him, please trust and believe, I would have him. And on that note... Malik, kiss your son bye. We will be back when your foul mouth girlfriend, who needs her mouth rinsed with soap, isn't here."

"Whatever, get home safe sweetie," I spat, taking the seat she just got up from.

She walked out shaking her head, but again, I could care less. She came for me when I didn't send for her ass.

"You need to check your son's mother, Malik."

Londyn

"Tamika, I told you that I'm not with her anymore, so you don't have to feel like you need to stake your claim every time you see her."

"So, you're taking her side?" I asked, not believing the words that just left his mouth.

"I'm just speaking the obvious, Tamika, so don't get mad at me because she sees the shit too. My mom already said you're too young for me and I defended your age; even saying how mature you are. So, don't prove me wrong with childish behavior."

"Wow! First off, your mother doesn't even acknowledge me when she visits, so I could give two shits how she or anyone else feels about me. I wouldn't have to feel a way if you stop that bitch from being up here every day. Your son is a year old, so he doesn't need to be up here in this germ filled hospital every day. I know it's just her ass wanting to see you. If you think otherwise, then you're not as smart as I thought you were or maybe you're just street smart," I insulted, not caring because he was talking her side.

"So, you're going to sit there and be disrespectful because you got called on your shit, Tamika? As far as my son being here every day, it shouldn't be any issue of yours because he's my son. So, if I don't have a problem with it, you shouldn't either. Also, when my parents walked in this room, they spoke to you. What more did you want from them? If my son and his mother being here bothers you, maybe you shouldn't come back to the hospital and just see me when I get up out of here."

"So, that's how you feel?" I asked on the verge of tears.

"Tamika, I'm not the one with the problem, you are. When you found out that I had a son, you decided to stay. So, to my understanding, you accepted it. If I'm wrong, I'm going to need you to let me know and we can part ways now, shorty."

I was trying to keep my tears at bay, but he was really hurting my feelings right now, like he didn't see his son mother start with me. And as far as his parents speaking when they were up here at the hospital; That's a damn lie. His mother rolled her eyes at me and his father sat on mute, so I have no idea what he's talking about. It's all good, though.

"I don't have a problem with your son, Malik, but I do have a problem with her being up here every day. Why do I have to share my time with her? Why she can't visit and take her ass home? She be up here from the afternoon until visiting hours are over. That's all I'm saying and trying to get you to understand. If I was laid up in the hospital, you wouldn't want my baby daddy, if I had one, up here all fucking day. Would you?"

"Nah, that nigga would have to bounce once he knew that you were good," he responded.

"That's exactly how I feel about your son's mom. She doesn't have to even bring him up here, if it's about your son visiting you then have your parent's bring him when they visit. " I tried to reason.

"I'll handle it, Tamika. Now come over here and give me a real kiss with your cry baby ass." he chuckled.

I got up to kiss him but something in my spirit was telling me that Malik wasn't being honest with me when it comes to his son's mother. I decided not to dwell on it. It could have been me thinking he guilty of something just because of my creeping with Aaron.

"Babe, I'm about to get on out of here because I'm tired. I was up all night, listening to the bullshit Q and Katrina has going on. Did you know that he was still fucking with that Jemima bitch?" I asked him.

"Now Tamika, you know I'm not getting in that man business just like he wouldn't get into mine," he responded.

Giving My Heart to A Gangsta

"Foul ass niggas stick together I see," I mumbled under my breath.

"What was that?" He asked.

"I didn't say anything," I lied.

As soon as I left the hospital, I took a cab to Aaron's house because I needed to relieve some stress. I would never admit it to Malik, but I was bothered by the relationship that he had with his son's mother and the fact that his parents didn't like me. I guess I was feeling his ass more than I cared to admit because I was wishing harm on his son's mother in my head.

Aaron was waiting in front of his building to pay for the cab with a sexy ass scowl on his face because I didn't want him to pick me up. I didn't want to argue about the reason I told him not to pick me up. I just want to be face down ass up on his bed while he ate my pussy from behind. Just thinking about what he was about to do to me had my body tingling all over.

Chapter Fourteen
(Katrina)

Tears fell from my eyes as Q penetrated me with his dick and I swear I was trying hard not to cry out from the pain. I closed my eyes and whimpered as he pushed inside of me with slow steady strokes. Although he was being gentle with me, it still hurt like hell.

"Are you ok? I could stop if you want me to," he said as he kissed my tears away.

"I'm ok," I lied.

I think he knew that I was lying because he pulled out of me. I thought he was mad at me until I felt his thick tongue devour the inside of my pussy. His tongue was dipping in and out of me while he allowed his fingers to rotate on my clit, sending a wave of wetness to gush out of me as my body shook uncontrollably. Just as my body began to calm, he pushed his dick back inside of me going strong with deep long strokes, causing me to lose my mind. I dug my nails into his back because the pain was intense, but the pleasure was intoxicating. I wrapped my legs around him and gyrated my hips into him.

Giving My Heart to A Gangsta

"Oh shit, I'm about to cum," he panted before grabbing my ass, pumping in and out of me again this time fast and hard until we came together.

I laid in the bed trying to catch my breath. Q was lightly snoring on his side of the bed, causing me to shake my head at his ass. I always thought after losing my virginity that I would feel different after hearing that you became a woman after having sex. Only thing I felt was a tingling throughout my body wanting him to do all the things that he did to me again and again until my ass couldn't walk. When I got up to go to the bathroom, I noticed blood on the sheets and started to panic because I didn't want him to see it. We were in the hotel room, so it wasn't like I could hide it with the pillow until he got up and quickly change the sheets. I had no choice but to leave it and hope that he wasn't disgusted by the site before me; I surely was. I went into the bathroom and closed the door locking it before calling Tamika to tell her that I was no longer a virgin.

"Hello," she answered sleepily.

"Tamika, are you sleeping?" I asked her.

"Just about, but it's ok. What's up?"

"I'm not a virgin anymore!" I sang happily into the phone.

Londyn

"What?" She questioned, no longer sounding sleepy.

"Yes girl, I finally did it," I smiled.

"Wait, I'm confused. I thought you were mad at his ass and you wasn't going to give it up until you were ready, Katrina?"

"Well, he didn't force me, Tamika. It just sorta happened. He took me to the Four Seasons Hotel and he wined and dined me in this beautiful room that I fell in love with. He apologized and promised me that if I agreed to be his girl, I wouldn't have to worry about him stepping out with any other females. It was just so romantic, and I got caught up in the moment. I was the one that got it popping because he was still willing to wait. He was so gentle with me even though it still hurt like hell. After a while, the feeling he gave my body was amazing. He's sleeping now and I'm hiding in the bathroom because when I got up, there was blood on the sheets. I'm so embarrassed," I told her.

"Nothing to be embarrassed about. Girl, it happens to all females after getting their cherry popped for the first time. Just go pick up the phone and have housekeeping bring up some more sheets or get your ass up and look around that expensive ass room because it might already be in there," she laughed.

Giving My Heart to A Gangsta

"It's still embarrassing, though," I told her before ending the call so that I could go look.

Tamika was right about this expensive ass room being stocked with everything that we needed so I didn't have to make the call. I tapped Q to wake him so that we could change the sheets. I had no reason to feel any way about the blood. He got up and removed the sheets without looking as if he was disgusted. After changing the bed, we showered together before calling it a night with me falling asleep in his arms.

The next morning during breakfast, he expressed that he really wanted my mother and I to accept his offer to move into the home in Queens. He said that he didn't have a problem putting all the paperwork in my mother's name, which was music to my ears, so I agreed. My mother and I already discussed it and that was the only condition that she had. Now that he said he would put her name on the paperwork, I was ready to move. He also said that since I agreed to be his girl, I shouldn't have to take the bus or wait on anyone to pick me up. He said the faster I learned how to drive and got my license, the faster I would have a car to call my own. I knew how to drive since the age of fourteen because my uncles were always letting me drive when I spent summers in North Carolina with them. I told him that I would start the process on Monday afterschool because I couldn't wait to see what kind of car he was going to get me. I swear his ass did and said all the right things. My mind was set to walk away at one point, but he got his second chance. I wasn't going to use him for his money like Tamika suggested. However, accepting his guilt gifts, I was going to do without a problem. We stayed at the hotel until noon the next day and although I wanted to stay longer, he had business to handle so he dropped me off at home. He said that he was going to start the paperwork on the house next week and once he had everything done, we would be able to move in. Just thinking about finally getting up out of the projects had me feeling like the luckiest person in the world. I was truly thankful for his kind offer to get us up out of here.

***

We have officially been living in our new home in Queens for a month, with Tamika and her mother living next door. My mom didn't have to come out of pocket for anything because Q allowed us to pick whatever we wanted to furnish the home and he picked up the tab. I was now driving a 2017 navy blue Altima that I picked out. For some reason, I have always wanted an Altima but never dreamed of having one while still in high school. Tamika hasn't even been in my new car yet. She's been distant for the past few days and I have no idea why. I was starting to think that she was jealous of my relationship with Q and how he's been spoiling me lately. Malik wasn't as generous as Q and I have no idea if that had to do with him having to take care of a son, but whatever was mine was hers without question. When I ordered my king-sized bedroom set from Ashley furniture, I ordered her a similar style and Q paid for both. Whenever he gave me cash, she was the one who I took to the mall to spend that cash with me. So, I hoped that her being distant had nothing to do with jealousy.

I went downstairs to knock on her door and when she answered, she didn't look like herself at all. Something was going on with my friend and I needed to know what it was. We were no longer living in the projects anymore, so she should have been wearing a permanent smile that matched mine; but she wasn't.

"Tamika, what's going on with you?" I asked her and for some reason, the question made her cry.

"Tamika, what's wrong? Why are you crying?" I pleaded with her because I was starting to worry.

"Katrina, I'm seventeen sleeping with two men and I just found out that I'm pregnant. I have no idea who fathered my child. I been up for two days trying to figure out what the hell

Londyn

I'm going to do because Aaron already has a child and expressed that he didn't want anymore. Malik has a son so he's probably not going to want another child either. I don't know how he's going to feel when I tell him that I'm pregnant and it might be his," she sobbed.

"Tamika, why didn't you tell me? You know I would have been here for you."

"I'm sorry, Katrina. I just been in a funk trying to process it. I need to tell my mother and I have no idea how she's going to feel. We just moved here, and a heavy burden was lifted. Now I have to tell her that her seventeen-year-old daughter is pregnant and has no idea who the father is," she said sadly.

"Tamika, trust me that it's going to be ok. Although she might be disappointed, I know she will never turn her back on you. I believe that whoever is the father of the baby, they will be willing to be here for you too," I tried to comfort her.

"I just don't want to see that disappointed look on her face when I tell her I don't know who the father is," she sniffed.

"So, don't tell her that you don't know who the father is because you do know that it's either Malik or Aaron's baby. Have you decided if you want to keep the baby being you're still in high school?" I asked her.

Giving My Heart to A Gangsta

"I don't know what I'm going to do right now because I didn't plan on getting pregnant," she responded. I was thinking like, what did she expect to happen while sleeping with two men unprotected?

I finally got her to calm down and when I told her what I thought was going on with her, she got really upset with me. She said she would never have any ill feelings towards me because she was my best friend and she loved me. She even went on to say that she was happy that Q was finally treating me the way that I deserved to be treated and she would never hate on that. I apologized to her for even thinking that she would do something like that to me knowing that she always had my back. I didn't stay long because I had to go pick up my aunt to take her to Wal-Mart. I swear that's the only thing I hated about having a car. Everybody wanted a damn ride somewhere.

I didn't mind spending time with my aunt today. It wasn't like I was going to see Q because he and Malik were out of town on business. My mom wasn't home because she's been spending all her free time with Q's uncle. According to him, he finally separated from his wife. I don't know if I believed him or not. My mom has been getting calls from private numbers a lot lately with the caller not saying anything. I told her that she shouldn't have started dating him until he showed her proof that he started the divorce process. I didn't want her falling in love just to get her heart broken. I went back inside to grab my car keys and phone that I heard ringing. I rushed to answer it because I knew that it was Q. The song *Favorite Pillow* from the movie Deuces was set as his ringtone because we were brand new lovers and the song fit our little romance we had going on. Not to mention, the fact that it mentions the Four Seasons hotel where I lost my virginity to him.

Chapter Fifteen
(Tamika)

"What's wrong with you, Malik?" I asked him. He hadn't been acting like himself since he picked me up from the house.

I didn't know what was up with him, but I was starting to have second thoughts about telling him that I was pregnant.

"I'm good. What have you been up to while I was gone?" He asked. The way he asked had me looking at him sideways.

"What do you mean what have I been doing?" I questioned his line of questioning.

"It's a simple fucking question, Tamika," he barked.

"I been going to school and right back home, Malik. Enough about that; I need to talk to you about something," I said to him.

Taking a deep breath, I just decided to tell him because he was starting to piss me off with how he was acting.

"Malik, I'm pregnant!" I blurted out.

Londyn

"By who?" He asked. I couldn't tell if he was joking or not because he was stone-faced.

"Are you being serious right now, Malik?"

"As serious as this ass whooping I'm going to put on your ass if you stand in my face and lie to me," he said as he fired up a blunt waiting on me to respond.

I don't know what happened on that trip of his, but he wasn't acting like himself and he was starting to scare me. I thought about telling him I wasn't feeling well and ask him if he could just take me home, but the look he was giving me let me know that I wasn't going anywhere until I answered his question.

"Malik, it's your baby," I stuttered.

"What the fuck did you just say?" He said, getting up.

He was now standing so close to me that I could smell the stench of the blunt he just had between his lips.

"I, I said it's your baby," I repeated, and he slapped me so hard that it felt like he broke my damn neck.

"Malik, why did you hit me?" I cried, holding my face and backing away from him.

Giving My Heart to A Gangsta

"I'm going to ask you again, Tamika, and you better answer me with the truth. Now, who are you pregnant by?"

I didn't say anything out of fear of being hit again. This was not the Malik I fell in love with because that Malik wouldn't have put his hands on me.

"I don't know what is going on with you, but I'm leaving," I attempted but he grabbed me by my neck and pushed me up against the wall, banging my head in the process.

I screamed out in pain, but it didn't faze him at all. The look in his eyes was murderous and I felt like I wasn't going to make it out of his house alive.

"Who else have you been fucking? My son's mother said that she saw you with some nigga while I was away so who the fuck was he, Tamika?" He snapped.

I was whimpering like a wounded dog because I knew if she saw me, it was Aaron who she saw me with. If she described him, then Malik already knew who I was with and he just wanted to hear me say it.

"I knew your hoe ass couldn't be trusted. And to think, I made your lying ass my girl!" He shouted before letting me go. "Tamika, I'm trying hard not to hurt you up in here, so you better tell me who the fuck that nigga was right now."

Londyn

He just slapped the shit out of me and yoked me up, slamming me against the wall, but he didn't want to hurt me? If that wasn't hurting me, I could only imagine what he was going to do to me once I told him that it was Aaron. Or when I tell him that Aaron could possibly be the father of the child that I'm carrying.

"I just want to go home!" I cried.

"You can go home after you tell me who the fuck Kashari saw you with and who the fuck you pregnant by," he repeated.

"I was with Aaron," I said, causing his jaw to tighten.

"So, that's Aaron's baby you're carrying?" He asked a little too calm for my taste.

"I, I don't know," I sniffed.

As soon as the words left my mouth, he slapped the shit out of me again, knocking me to the floor this time. All I could do was try my best to cover myself as he kicked and punched me like I was some dude in the streets until he got tired. I stayed on the floor for what seemed like hours after he left slamming the door behind him. I was in so much pain as I crawled over to my bag taking my phone out to call Katrina to come pick me up. I was embarrassed, hurt and confused as to how he could do something like this to me and just leave me on that cold as floor in pain.

Katrina was livid. She called Q and told him she was going to take Malik's fucking life when she saw him. I could tell that he was trying to get a word in, but she was on ten and when she was done threatening his friend, she ended the call. When I got home, I told her that I was going to be ok, so she told me to call her if I needed her. I went into the bathroom to run me a bath so that I could soak my body because I was in a lot of pain. I cried myself to sleep that night. Malik hurt me mentally and physically. I would never have expected that reaction from his ass. I saw a side of him that now made me pray that I wasn't pregnant by him because I was done with him. I refuse to be with a man that could put his hands on me without so much as enough restraint to just walk away. I was wrong, but he had no right putting his hands on me. I didn't put my hands on his ass when I found out about Nicola.

Aaron has been calling my phone, but I wasn't ready to talk to him. I ignored the call and continued to nurse my face with ice. The redness and swelling were still the same because I didn't put ice on it that same night. I stayed home from school. When I heard the knock at the door, I thought it was Katrina coming to check on me, but it was Aaron. I now regretted having him drop me off at home last week. I was able to hide my face from my mom by talking to her from my room, but I knew if I let him in, he was going to see it.

"Tamika, I know you're inside so just open the door," he demanded.

As soon as I opened the door and he looked at me, concern graced his face as he caressed the side of my face that was swollen.

"What happened to your face, Tamika?" He questioned, causing me to burst into tears.

He grabbed my hand and walked me over to the couch while looking me in my face, waiting for me to say something.

"Aaron, I'm sorry," I cried.

"Sorry for what?" He asked, confused.

I put my face into my hands and cried my heart out. I didn't want to hurt him, but I knew I needed to tell him the truth.

"Tamika," he called out as he touched my shoulder gently. "Talk to me, Tamika." he said as he removed my hands from my face.

Giving My Heart to A Gangsta

I looked in his eyes knowing he deserved the truth, so I took a deep breath, praying that he didn't hurt me the way Malik did when I tell him.

"Aaron, I was still seeing Malik at the same time I was seeing you and I'm pregnant," I admitted as my body shook.

I closed my eyes because I was scared to look at him or see the slap or punch that never came. I opened my eyes to look at him and it hurt me to see the hurt in his eyes.

"I'm sorry," I whispered as the tears continued falling from my eyes.

When he touched me, I jumped until he pulled me into his arms holding me until my body stopped shaking. That's how scared I was that he was going to hit me the same way Malik did. But, he was calm about what I just told him.

"So, did Malik do this to your face?" He asked me, and I nodded my head.

I felt his body tense up, so I kept repeating how sorry I was as he continued to hold me in his arms.

"Did he touch you anywhere else?" He asked me.

After I told him everything that happened at Malik's house, I could tell that he was upset but he didn't say anything.

149

Londyn

"Look, I have to go, but I'm going to need you to make a doctor's appointment so that we can make sure that everything is good with the baby. Ok?" He asked, kissing my lips.

"Ok," I responded, letting him out.

After he left, I sat on the couch letting the tears fall. The one person that really cared about me... I hurt him for the second time and he still was here for me. Katrina told me that I was playing a dangerous game and I should have listened to her. If I had, I wouldn't have gotten my ass kicked. I called Katrina to let her know that I was ok before she decided to stop by because I didn't want that to happen. I just wanted to be alone and left to my thoughts as I tried to figure out what I wanted to do as far as my pregnancy. If this baby didn't belong to Aaron, I didn't want to have it. I be damned if I wanted to deal with Malik 'sass for the next eighteen years. I climbed in my bed and decided to give my thoughts a rest as I closed my eyes and tried to make all the pain and heartache disappear. I knew this was just the beginning.

I don't know how long I was asleep, but I was being awakened by my mother and I knew that I was going to have to tell her something. I looked over at the time on the clock and noticed that she was home early so that probably meant she already knew what was going on. If Katrina told her mother, most likely she already had a conversation with my mother, but I wasn't even mad.

Chapter Sixteen
(Quentin)

"My nigga, that was some sucker shit you did to that girl and you need to apologize to her," I told Malik's ass. I swear, if he wasn't my boy, I would fuck him up for that bullshit.

"I don't know what happened, man. I just snapped knowing that she was still fucking with that lame ass nigga. Now she's pregnant and she doesn't know if the baby belongs to me or him. So, like I said, I snapped," he tried.

"Well. it doesn't matter if it's your baby or not because she doesn't want nothing to do with your ass," I told him.

He got Katrina mad as shit at me because she was on some guilty by association shit when I would never put my hands on a female unless it was necessary. Now he was sitting here thinking someone was going to feel sorry for his ass because Tamika's not taking any of his calls. He was trying to apologize but she wasn't trying to hear nothing he had to say, and I didn't blame her. She talked her mother out of pressing charges against his ass so if I was him, I would just leave well enough alone.

152

Giving My Heart to A Gangsta

"Let's get up out of here. You're depressing the shit out of me," I told his ass.

We decided to go hug the block and shoot craps with them niggas that always seemed to be fucking around instead of getting this money. I gave their asses a pass just because I was trying to get Malik up out of the funk that he was in. One thing's for sure and two things for certain, when this dice game was over, I was getting in these niggas' ass. I'm about my business and that's the same way I needed these niggas to be. So, if they're all about fun and games, it's time to get some real trap niggas that's about making money. I bent down to grab the dice when I saw movement, but these motherfuckers weren't paying attention to their surroundings. I was always on point and so was my nigga Malik.

"So, you like hitting females? Try putting your hands on me, nigga," Aaron barked at Malik.

I swear if Aaron wasn't serious, the shit would be comical right now. One would have never taken him as that nigga to be running up on anyone. We already beat his ass at the cabin, so for him to be here ready to go to war knowing that most likely we were strapped, it impressed me. I stood back just to see how the shit was going to play out. Malik needed his ass kicked for putting his hands on that girl.

Londyn

"Don't stand there acting like I didn't already beat that ass," Malik told him, but Aaron wasn't fazed. Last time, he was out numbered but this time, he had like four niggas with him.

"Try that shit now, my nigga," Aaron told him, removing his flight jacket.

Just as Malik went to remove his jacket, Aaron landed a punch that knocked Malik cold the fuck out before stepping off like he was that nigga. I could do nothing but respect his gangsta. I helped my nigga up off the ground, trying not to clown his ass with the rest of those niggas. The last time I jumped in because he was drunk. Had Aaron's niggas jumped in, I would have bodied something but none of that popped off. I guess Malik didn't understand my position because he snatched away from me and walked off after saying, "Fuck all you niggas." I knew that he was just in his feelings, so I let that slick shit fly, telling those niggas to get back to work before leaving the block.

I called Katrina and told her that I was coming to scoop her up. I missed my girl and wanted to spend some time with her. She came outside looking cute, wearing a green flight jacket and some ripped jeans with a green pair of Huaraches on. I told her that I didn't like the sneakers when she picked them out, but they looked nice on her small feet. She got in the car and planted a kiss on my lips before leaning back over and putting her seatbelt on. I was happy that she was no longer mad at me for that sucker shit that Malik did to her girl. I guess she realized that she was taking that shit out on the wrong person.

"How was your day?" She asked.

"Comical," I chuckled, thinking about Malik getting handled by Aaron.

"What made it comical?" She asked.

"That nigga Malik and I was chilling on the block when Aaron walked up with like four dudes flexing on Malik for hitting Tamika. I stood back and watched what was going to happen as they talked shit. Aaron removed his jacket and didn't even give Malik a chance to remove his. He hit him with one punch and knocked my nigga out cold," I laughed.

"That's what his ass gets," she laughed.

"I helped his ass up off the ground, but he was mad those niggas were clowning and mad at my ass for not helping. When I got involved last time, it was because he was drunk and couldn't defend himself, but that shit was a one on one. Had those niggas jump in, I would have bodied something and to be honest, he deserved that shit for hitting a female like that," I admitted.

"He better be lucky Aaron served his ass because I had something for his punk ass when I saw him," she spat.

"I see you gangsta, huh?" I joked.

"I'm not a gangsta. I just don't like that sucker shit he pulled."

"I let him know that he was dead wrong for that shit and needed to make it right."

"She doesn't want his apology. He just needs to stay away from her because he's not dealing with a full deck the way he did her. She could care less if he is the father of her baby; she just wants to be left alone. I don't understand why he mad when I'm sure she wasn't the only female he was smashing," she said but I wasn't even going to respond to that last part.

"So, what do you want to eat?" I asked, changing the subject.

"I have to be to school in the morning so whatever we get, it has to be something quick. I have a paper that I need to hand in that I didn't even start, so I'll be up all night working on it.

"I wanted us to spend some time together, shorty."

Giving My Heart to A Gangsta

"I know but it will have to be this weekend. You know if I spend the night at your house I'm not going to get my paper done," she laughed.

It was true because the last time she stayed over, she didn't even make it to school the next day, so she knew that I wasn't going to leave her alone to do her paper. I pulled up to McDonald's drive thru and her face lit up. That's what I loved about her. The simplest things make her happy, letting me know that she wasn't with me for my money. Jemima's ass would have had her nose turned all the way up if I tried to take her to McDonalds like she wasn't a damn hood rat.

"Welcome to McDonald's. What can I get for you?"

"Can I get a number five with a coke, no ice and let me have the big mac, a six-piece nugget with mac sauce in a cup and a sweet tea."

I looked over at Katrina who was smiling all wide and shit because I remembered her order from the last time we were here. I only remembered what she ordered because of her dipping her nuggets in that nasty ass mac sauce. After getting our order, I drove back to her house and we sat out in the car eating, talking and enjoying each other company until she questioned me about my parents. My mood shifted instantly causing me to shut down, I wasn't trying to have that conversation with her.

"I have to go. I'll call you before I crash tonight," I told her.

"I'm sorry, I didn't mean to pry," she apologized.

"No need to apologize, shorty. I'm just not ready to talk about it," I told her, kissing her lips.

"I understand," she responded, returning the kiss before getting out of the car.

I knew that she didn't understand and was feeling a way that she knew nothing about me beside my being in the streets and my uncle. Shit was complicated, and I just wasn't ready to share that part of my life with her right now. I stopped at the liquor store and I was now parked in the hood, taking the Hennessey to the head straight from the bottle. The mere mention of my parents always took me to a place that I didn't want to go, so the liquor took me from my dark thoughts.

I heard a knock on the passenger side window. Seeing that it was Jemima, I popped the locks and she hopped her ass in.

"What do you want, Jemima?" I barked.

Giving My Heart to A Gangsta

"I just wanted to make sure that you were good being you were just sitting in your car," she said, touching my leg.

My dick instantly got hard and I didn't know if the liquor had me reacting to her or my ass was turned on by her touch. Her hand was now massaging my dick though my jeans, causing me to push her hand away. I wasn't trying to go there with her ass. She wasn't taking me seriously, and my dick being brick hard didn't convince her that I wasn't enjoying her touch. She had my dick out of my pants and in her mouth. All I could do was lay my head back and enjoy her sucking the shit out of my dick. I grabbed her head as she bobbed up and down on my shit while I pumped in and out of her mouth until I released in her mouth.

"Q, put the seat back," she demanded.

I knew that I should have kicked her ass out once I bust my nut, but I wanted some pussy, so I put the seat back and she straddled my lap. She was riding my dick like she knew this would be the last time and she should have because this was going to be the last time. I grabbed her hips helping her as she gyrated her hips into me, causing me to growl out. Her pussy felt so fucking good and I was hating how she had a nigga feeling. I promised Katrina that I wasn't going to touch this girl again and here I was balls deep in her shit, forgetting that I had a fucking girl.

The liquor had my judgment clouded as I stuck my tongue in her mouth kissing her passionately like she was my bitch. She started to slow grind on my dick, panting that she loved me, and my ass told her that I loved her too, knowing that I was bent off that Hennessey. I grabbed her ass and continued to fuck the shit out of her until she screamed that she was cumming before sticking her tongue back into my mouth. I slapped her on the ass and told her to climb in the backseat because I was ready to hit from the back. She did exactly what I told her, and I was banging the shit out of her pussy. Again, I knew that the liquor had me in a zone as I fucked her without a care in the world. I nutted all up in her like she was my girl as I pulled her hair pumping all my seeds into her before pulling out and collapsing against the seat. She collapsed leaning against me trying to catch her breath, but I told her to put her shit on and get the fuck out of my car. I know that I shouldn't have blamed her because I was at fault to. That bitch knew that I had a girl, so she should have never put my dick in her mouth. She saw that I was gone off that Hennessey and took advantage, knowing that I wasn't going to stop her once she pulled my shit out.

Giving My Heart to A Gangsta

"So, it's like that Q? If it's like that you should have said the shit before I had your dick in my mouth. I just don't understand why we keep playing these games, you know that I love you and you love me too. You need to leave that little young girl alone and be with me like you said you would before meeting her ass. I don't understand how you even started something with her knowing that you were still very much in a relationship with me."

"Listen, I was drunk as shit so whatever I did or said, was because I was under the influence. You must have been drinking too because you're being delusional right now. I don't know how many times I have to tell you that we were never in a relationship. We were nothing more than fuck buddies until you fucked that up."

"Fuck buddies, Q. Really?" She asked as the tears fell from her eyes.

I watched as she aggressively grabbed her jacket and bag, getting out of my car and slamming my door with so much force I thought she cracked my window. I felt like snapping her fucking neck, but I wasn't about to make a scene in the hood and the shit get back to my shorty. I took my ass home and crashed on the sofa, feeling like shit knowing that I fucked up and cheated on Katrina again. If she found out, she would leave me for good this time and nothing I said to her would change her mind.

I woke up the next morning with a banging headache and feeling like shit as I dragged myself off the couch to go take a shower. It was almost noon so that Henny knocked me on my ass because I never slept this late in the day. I grabbed my phone to call Katrina to see if she finished her paper last night, knowing that she should be on her lunch period. I saw that I had like ten missed calls from her and I just prayed that she wasn't calling about the shit I did last night with Jemima.

Chapter Seventeen
(Tamika)

I sat in my living room across from Aaron shooting daggers his way because I was pissed right now with him. I didn't ask him to defend me by stepping to Malik even though that nigga needed to be handled. I just feel that Aaron should have left it alone because he just made the situation worse. I'm not sure if he did it on my behalf or if he did it on some jealous shit being I was still fucking with them both.

"Why are you looking at me like that?" He finally questioned with a scowl on his face.

"I'm looking at you like this because I'm pissed that you stepped to Malik when I didn't ask you to, Aaron," I stated, releasing a frustrated sigh.

"So, that nigga put his hands on you and you thought I was going to let that shit slide? I see you got me fucked up. I don't understand why you're upset unless you still trying to be with his lame ass. Is that it, Tamika? You still trying to be with him?"

Londyn

"It has nothing to do with me trying to be with him. It has to do with you making the situation worse. Do you think that Malik is just going to take that sucker punch and do nothing?" I asked him.

"Sucker punch? Wow, so who the fuck you been listening to because I didn't sucker punch that nigga. I cold laid his ass out, so fuck what you heard," he barked.

I wasn't trying to upset him, but I wanted him to understand that the type of nigga Malik is, he wasn't going to let the shit slide. I didn't want anything to happen to either of them because I cared for them both. I'm angry with Malik right now and don't want shit to do with him; that doesn't mean I want harm to come to him. I don't care who doesn't understand why I still care about his wellbeing.

"Look, Aaron, I'm not trying to upset you. I don't want you to think that I'm defending him, because I'm not. I don't want him retaliating and something happens to you when this wasn't your beef to begin with," I tried to reason.

"Trust when I say that I'm not worried about that nigga the same way you shouldn't be worried about him. You're sitting here saying that you're not defending him but that's what it sounds like to me. He put hands on you and left you all fucked up knowing that you're pregnant so you're looking real stupid right now even questioning me about his ass."

I wasn't going to say shit else because he wasn't getting where I was coming from and I was done trying to explain it to him.

"So, you don't have shit to say, Tamika? Well, let me be the first to tell you that the nigga doesn't give a shit about you. He's a grimy ass nigga and you saw the shit for yourself. So, if you trying to forgive him let me know now. Also, I need to know where he stands with you if this baby turns out to be his?" He questioned, causing me to roll my eyes at him.

I still didn't say shit because I didn't know what he wasn't saying about Malik. He was sounding like he knew something but refused to go into details. If this was his way of warning me, I wasn't with it. If he knew something, he needed to say it. I wasn't going to even ask him to elaborate because as soon as I did, he was going to accuse me of still caring about him and the argument would never end.

"Can we not talk about Malik anymore?" I pleaded.

"I didn't come here to talk about that nigga. You started that conversation, Tamika. I came over to check on you and find out if you made the appointment to make sure everything is good with the baby."

"I made the appointment for tomorrow, Aaron," I answered dryly.

"So, how are you feeling?" He asked, but I was no longer in the mood to talk.

"I see that you're in your feelings so I'm out. I'll call you later to get the appointment time so that I can pick you up tomorrow," he said before leaving out pissed.

I'm not going to lie and say he didn't leave me in my feelings being I was tight right now. He knew in his heart that him going after Malik was for his own personal feelings, but he tried to act as if he did it for him putting his hands on me. I heard the faint knock on the door and knew that it was his ass coming back with his tail between his legs to apologize. One thing I could say about him, if he felt he was wrong, he would apologize and not wait weeks later to let me know.

I opened the door, ready to tell him that I was sorry too, but it was Malik standing on the other side of the door. I wanted to bark at him for having the audacity to be standing at my door after what he did to me, but I just stood frozen. I don't know if it was out of fear or what, but my body went stiff on my ass until he spoke, spitting bullshit out his mouth.

"So, now you fucking the nigga in the spot I made possible for your hoe ass?" He barked, pushing passed me.

"Who I fuck or where I fucked them is no longer any concern of yours, Malik. So, please leave!" I shouted finding my voice.

"No longer any concern of mine? When it *was* a concern of mine, it didn't stop you from still fucking the nigga, so what's the difference now? I'll tell you what the difference is since you seem to be having trouble comprehending what I'm trying to state to you. I took you and your mother out of that piss smelling housing project that you called home, so I be damned if you're going to fuck the nigga that you were cheating on me with in the spot I paid for."

I released a deep breath trying hard not to let tears of frustration fall because between the argument with Aaron and now this with him they both had me regretting fucking with either of them. I understood both their position on how they were feeling right now but my state of mind wasn't in a state to give a fuck at this point I just wanted to be left alone. I didn't want to argue, be questioned, explain my actions or my reasons to anyone right now. I was pregnant with a baby that I didn't know who the father is or if I even wanted to carry the baby to term. So, like I said I just wanted to be left the fuck alone.

My chest started to heave up and down as the tears fell from my eyes causing him to walk into my personal space pulling me into his arms. I wanted to push him away, but I just sobbed into his chest, wishing that everything could have went back to the way it was. I was wrong for cheating on him and he was wrong for putting his hands on me. I wished us both apologizing to each other would make it better, but I knew it wouldn't. Aaron was now in the equation and I still cared for him just as much as I still cared for Malik.

"I'm sorry," he whispered in my ear.

"I didn't mean to hurt you, Tamika. I let my feelings get the best of me finding out another nigga touched you."

"I'm sorry too, Malik," I said to him.

Just as he was about to kiss me, the knock on the door interrupted his lips from connecting with mine. My eyes grew wide as I saw Aaron standing at my door with the same scowl on his face that he left with earlier. I should have known he was going to come back to apologize or to at least talk about our argument. I was petrified at the thought of Malik being inside, knowing that Aaron saw his car parked in front of my house.

"What is he doing here, Tamika?" He questioned with dark eyes and venom in his voice.

"He, he just came by to apologize, Aaron," I stuttered nervously.

I prayed that Malik didn't come to the door, but I knew that he would, being he felt he had something to prove. When I felt his presence behind me, my body shook from the fear of the two of them getting into it again. Malik pushed me behind him and he was now standing face to face with Aaron. I just knew that this wasn't going to end without someone getting hurt.

"Nigga, you need to bounce," Malik barked at him.

"Fuck that shit you spitting. This is my girl crib, so you need to bounce," Aaron retorted.

I wanted to intervene, but my ass was conflicted as to which one I was going to ask to leave being I was seeing them both. I loved the them both, so I knew that whichever one I asked to leave, the other was going to be in their feelings.

Londyn

"Tamika, let this nigga know to get up out of here," Malik demanded, never turning around.

I guess he wasn't giving Aaron another chance to sucker punch him again which I totally understood. Aaron's eyes met mine, causing me to lower my head because I had no idea what to do, knowing I didn't want to hurt either of them.

"I think that both of you need to go before my mother gets home," I said, praying that they would just leave at the sound of my mother coming home.

"Nah, fuck that, Tamika. You need to choose who the fuck you trying to be with," Aaron snapped.

"She's going to be with the nigga who seed she's carrying so that eliminates your punk ass," Malik shot off.

"Oh, so that's your seed? Last I checked, I was raw knee deep all up in the pussy," Aaron boasted, and I felt disrespected by his statement.

I guess Malik felt some way about his statement as well because he hauled off and punched the shit out of Aaron; they started fighting. I didn't know what to do because they both were in beast mode. All I knew to do was call to see if Katrina was home so that she could come help me with these niggas. I was scared to even try to break them up because I'm pregnant and didn't need to be getting hit by one of them. They were handling each other, both trying to prove something. I was aggravated to the point that I was ready to throw some fucking hot water on their asses. I'd never been so happy to see Katrina in my life and when she walked in with Q's uncle, I was so damn thankful. He was able to separate them and get Malik to leave the house with him. At this point, I was just trying to stop my tears from falling.

Aaron left out in his feelings, slamming the door again on his way out and making me realize that the situation is way out of hand. I had no idea what to do to fix it. Katrina was looking at me like she wanted to punch me in my face for even having Malik in my space again. She didn't understand that turning off feelings wasn't something that I was able to do overnight just because I was upset with him.

"Why the fuck was Malik here, Tamika? I told you that you're playing a dangerous game that's going to get Aaron killed. If you care about him like you say, then be with him or let him go because this shit is getting out of hand. Malik violated you and you still fucking with him. What the fuck is wrong with you?"

Londyn

"Katrina, I didn't know he was going to show up here so stop fucking yelling at me," I cried so ready to just disappear from it all.

"I'm yelling at you because this could have been a murder scene right now and you're not understanding that. I don't give a fuck what Malik paid for. All the paperwork is in your mother's name which means he has no right to be here if you don't want him here," she stressed.

When Q's uncle told him to leave, he was yelling about how he didn't have to leave because he paid for this house so that's what she was referring to. I wanted to tell her that he didn't force his way into my house because I invited him in, but I was done arguing about it. Now that Malik and Aaron were out, I wanted her out too; I just wanted to be alone with my thoughts. I was really considering going away to college after I graduate because running seemed like the solution to my problems right now. She just looked at me and when I didn't say anything else, she rolled her eyes and walked out. I locked my door behind her, not giving a fuck what she thought right now. I had to worry about my mother going off about them fucking up her living room, so I was trying to clean up as much as I could, but how was I going to explain the broken television amongst other things.

172

Giving My Heart to A Gangsta

After straightening up and salvaging anything that was able to be salvaged, I went upstairs to take a shower. My head was banging, and my stomach was cramping a little, so I took two Tylenols praying that it made me feel a little better. My phone was ringing so I went into the bathroom to retrieve it off the sink and I saw that it was Aaron calling. I didn't want to answer the call, but I felt that I needed to explain to him why Malik was here. As soon as I said 'hello', he told me to open the door. When I opened the door, I saw the 50" television sitting on the porch. However, he wasn't there, which led me to believe that he was blaming me for what went down, causing tears to fall from my eyes.

Chapter Eighteen
(Quentin)

"Nigga, you need to get your head in the fucking game and stop stressing that Tamika and Aaron bullshit. If she wants to be with that nigga, let the shit be. Stop acting like your ass not still smashing Nicola," I told his ass.

"Fuck that shit, Q. I'm not about to let that bitch play me after dropping stacks for her and her fucking mother to live comfortably. She had that nigga chilling in the crib on some disrespectful shit."

"Bruh, I don't have time for this soap opera romance you got going on, my nigga. We have a shipment of those guns coming in tonight, so I need you on your A game. You out here beefing with a nigga when shorty the one playing mind games with the both of you dumb asses. I need you to suck that shit up and let's get this money," I told him, ending the conversation.

"We're linking up with these niggas at eight, so I need you to have your cash and be ready to meet me at the spot by seven," I confirmed for his ass.

Giving My Heart to A Gangsta

"I got you nigga," he said, giving me dap before heading out.

I really needed him on his game because I already had buyers for this first shipment. I need my team of niggas and my right-hand man focused.

Malik had my ass vexed. Every time he got into it with Tamika, Katrina be on her bullshit, taking it out on me. I keep telling her ass that Malik is my dude, but his actions are no reflection on me and she needed to understand that. She straight acting like I put hands on her or fucked up her mom's living room to the point I had to hang up the phone on her ass. She wanted to argue about shit that didn't have shit to do with us. I needed to relieve some stress before handling this business, so I had Jemima on the way over. I was trying to be that man she wanted me to be, but she stayed bitching; something that I didn't have the energy to keep doing. If it was my fuck up, I would sit and take it. But, I was getting chewed out for another man fuck up and I wasn't with that shit.

Jemima showed up about forty-five minutes later looking sexy as shit, causing my shit to brick up ready for whatever. Jemima didn't care how many times I disrespected her or played her ass to the left; she always came when I called. Last time she told me she wasn't fucking with me anymore, but her ass was standing here willing and waiting. I guess we both lied to ourselves every chance that we got. I told her ass that she wouldn't get anymore of this dick, but here I was, holding my shit, ready for her to put her lips to it. She wasted no time getting on her knees removing my dick from my sweats and taking my brick hard dick into her mouth. I grabbed her head pumping in and out of her mouth aggressively, taking my frustrations out on her mouth. She played with my balls getting me to calm down. I moaned out in pleasure as she now jerked my dick and sucked my balls at the same time. Just as I was about to cum, she put my dick back in her mouth, catching every drop before coming up out of her clothes.

I bent her ass over the couch, fucking her until her legs gave out on her and she was trying to tap out. I had at least one more nut in me, so I sat on the couch and pulled her on top of me.

"Ride this dick," I told her, slapping her on the ass.

I pounded into her so hard at the thought of Katrina curving me on some bullshit when she should have been the one taking this dick.

Giving My Heart to A Gangsta

"Q, slow down; you're hurting me," she whined as I held on to her hips, digging in her pussy with deep long strokes until I growled, releasing all my seeds inside of her.

I pushed her up off me before laying my head against the sofa with my eyes closed and feeling a way about fucking up again. My eyes opened to Jemima kneeling in front of me wiping me with a warm cloth, but it wasn't necessary. I was about to hop in the shower to get ready to handle this business and I hope she wasn't going to be on no bullshit.

"Do you want to order something to eat and watch a movie?" She asked, getting up.

"Nah, I got some business to handle in about an hour, so I have to shower and get ready to handle that. I'll get up with you though," I told her, causing her facial expression to change.

"So, if you knew that you had something to do, why didn't you have me come over after your business was done? We never get to chill after we fuck, Q, and that shit starting to make me feel like that's all you want from me," she responded, getting on her delusional shit again.

Londyn

"Jemima, why you always act like you don't know what this shit is? You know I have a girl, so why you always trying to make it something that it's not?"

"You know how I feel about you so why do you keep calling me if you know that you have a girl and not trying to be with me? I don't understand how you just played me to the left and started seeing this bitch and treating me like a trick. We used to chill all the time without a problem and it wasn't just about sex either," she spat.

"I'm not about to do this with you right now, Jemima. I told you that I have business to handle," I tried not to get pissed.

"So, go handle your business and I'll be here when you get back," she tried.

"Jemima, I'll call you if I don't get back to late. I'm not leaving you in my crib until I get back like you're my girl or some shit."

"I don't know why I keep doing this shit to myself," she said to herself as she put her clothes on.

She left out without saying anything to me, but I didn't feel any way about it. She needed to stop acting like she didn't know that we were just fucking. I went upstairs and took a shower before getting dressed in all black, making sure that I was strapped for whatever. I hoped the shit went as planned without any snake shit or fuck ups because I didn't have a problem murking a nigga tonight.

Business went according to plan, so we decided that we were going to hang out at the club tonight to celebrate. I didn't really want to hang out because Katrina has yet to take any of my calls or texts, pissing me off. What I really wanted to do was show up to her crib and force her ass to talk to me and tell me what her fucking problem was. I was getting so sick and tired of being the one to apologize to her ass when I didn't do shit to begin with. Well, at least nothing she knows about. Jemima started blowing me up, but I wasn't about to sit in the crib on a Friday night watching movies and eating out unless it was with my girl. I showered again and changed my clothes before heading out to meet up with Malik and my dudes at the club.

You get the bag and fumble it, I get the bag and flip it and tumble it.

Straight out the lot, three hundred cash and the car came with a blunt in it.

Londyn

We walked into the club to the DJ spinning Gucci Mane's *I Get the Bag* with the crowd going crazy singing the lyrics.

"This shit is lit tonight," I said to Malik over the music as we made our way to VIP.

"Hey Malik," Nicola smiled, walking up with two bad ass females.

"What's up," Malik responded with a head nod.

"Eww, why are you acting all stink and shit?" She asked with a roll of her eyes.

"Yo, I just came to chill so move around," he barked, walking away and leaving her with an embarrassed look on her face.

He was in his feelings about Tamika and I was in mine. I pulled out a rolled up blunt from earlier, so we could get right. I downed two shots of Hennessey before taking a few pulls on the blunt and passing it to his ass. Nicola was not one to be disrespected because she invited herself and her friends to VIP after he told her to move around. Shorty rocking the bright red braids was looking good as shit to a nigga right now. She was a light skin cutie rocking some tight ass jeans that had her ass sitting up just right causing a nigga dick to get hard.

Giving My Heart to A Gangsta

"What's up, shorty? What's your name?" I asked her.

She had some light brown eyes that complimented her smile along with some nice ass lips that had my ass thinking what that mouth gone do.

"My name is Londyn, and yours?" She responded, taking me from my nasty thoughts of her.

"I'm Q," I told her, inviting her to sit next to me so that I could holla at her.

Malik was having a lover's spat with Nicola and my nigga Ant wasted no time kicking it to her other homegirl. I chilled with Londyn and the more shots she took back, the more comfortable she got being she was acting shy beforehand. She was only visiting for the weekend and had to be back to Georgia State University where she goes to school. Nicola was her cousin and not her friend like I originally thought, which was a good thing because I was really feeling shorty. I wanted to spend some time with her before she had to head back to school, so hopefully she's going to be cool with it since her cousin is chilling with Malik. His ass loosened up because she was sitting in his lap while he played up under her skirt, forgetting all about Tamika's ass.

Londyn

"So, are you trying to chill with a nigga for the weekend?" I asked her to see if she was feeling me the same way I was feeling her.

"I don't know about the weekend, but I'm good with chilling with you tonight," she responded shyly.

"Say no more," I told her before dapping my niggas up and letting Nicola know that her cousin was good before heading out of the club.

Being Jemima was blowing my phone up all night and I wasn't responding, I took Londyn to the hotel. Jemima, without a doubt, would have done a pop-up on my ass. Although I didn't have to explain shit to her, I wasn't about to have her scare Londyn off before I got to smash.

I swear I shouldn't have been thinking about Jemima's ass because as quickly as I thought of her, she was sending me another text message. They had stopped about an hour ago, so I figured that she took her ass to bed. *I guess not,* I thought, looking at the message before pulling out.

Jemima- It doesn't look like you're handling business to me, but it's all good, Q. Enjoy your night.

I don't know what she meant but I deleted the message and headed toward the Marriot, not giving her ass a second thought.

Giving My Heart to A Gangsta

Londyn and I spent the night smoking, drinking and fucking. When I tell you that she had a nigga tapping out, I tapped out. They always say that the quiet ones are freaks, and they hit that shit on the nail with her ole freaky ass. We'd just finished getting dressed so that I could take her to Nicola's crib and when we got to my car, I was pissed the fuck off. Someone fucked my shit up.

Chapter Nineteen
(Jemima)

Q has played with my feelings for the last fucking time with his bitch ass thinking that he's God gift to females, so he can treat them anyway he feels. Not. I accepted the fact that he was claiming Katrina's ass, but I be damned if he was going to play me to the left with a random bitch he just met. I was sitting outside of his house when he came back from handling business being he said that we could chill when he got back. Imagine my surprise when he ignored my calls and text but came out of the house looking good as fuck, getting in his car to leave. I decided to follow him, figuring that he was going to that bitch Katrina's crib. Nope, this nigga was going to the fucking club. I thought about leaving but I decided to wait him out. When I saw him leave the club with a bitch, my feelings were hurt. I sent the text message and that was going to be it, but my curiosity got the best of me and I wanted to see if he was just dropping her off at home.

When he pulled up to the Marriot, my anger replaced the hurt I was feeling in that moment, making me want to cry but I didn't. I slashed his tires and broke out all his fucking windows, not giving a shit if he knew it was me or not. I knew that he had an idea that it was me because he was now blowing my phone up, but I wasn't going to answer. Fuck him.

I grabbed my phone and my bag to leave to head to my bestie house, but as soon as I opened the door, I was punched in the face. Q bust my shit wide open as the blood poured from my nose.

"Bitch, if you ever in your fucking life touch something that belongs to me, I will snap your neck and not give a fuck. I don't know how many times you have to hear me say stay in your lane when dealing with me. You made the choice to continue fucking with me knowing that I wasn't going to wife your ass or even be with you on any level besides us fucking," he barked.

"Q, you're a fucking liar because you not only told me we were going to be together, we were together. You started fucking with that bitch Katrina, upgraded her to girlfriend and downgraded me to a fuck buddy without so much as an explanation. So, miss me with the bullshit," I told him, now using my shirt to clean the blood from my face.

Londyn

I stood in my bra and his eyes were fixated on my breast, causing me to shake my head because this nigga didn't know what the fuck he wanted.

"Stop looking at me like you didn't just punch me in my fucking face, nigga. You best believe that you will never hit this pussy again!" I yelled at him.

"What the fuck you just say to me?" He snapped, grabbing me by my neck and pushing me against the wall.

"Play with me if you want, Jemima. This is my fucking pussy and I'll run up in it whenever I feel like I want to give you the dick. If I even hear that you in a nigga face trying to give him my pussy, I'm going to bury you and that nigga."

He grabbed my pussy aggressively, finger fucking me through my jeans and causing me to moan out like he didn't just bust my shit.

"Bitch, come up out of those fucking jeans," he demanded, and I obliged.

When he got on his knees and put his head between my legs, all was forgiven as he bit down on my clit before sucking. It was so much pressure that I came within seconds. I just didn't understand my obsession to keep dealing with his disrespect and allowing him to fuck me whenever he wanted to when I knew that I wasn't the only one that he was fucking. After he had his way with me, he threatened me by saying that every time I touch something that he cared about he was going to touch something that I cared about; whatever that meant.

I had my back against the wall with my knees up, crying my eyes out. Once again, I did nothing to stop his mental and physical abuse. He said that he would never put his hands on a female, so I guess my fucking up his car took him over the top. I didn't know why he was acting like he didn't have about three other cars that he could drive. The ringing of my phone forced me up from my pity party to answer the call because it was Tierra calling and I needed someone to talk to.

"Hey girl, I know that I'm supposed to have been there by now, but Q's ass came here bugging about what I did to his car," I rambled.

"Jemima, this is Tierra's mom."

"I'm sorry, Ms. Lynch," I apologized, feeling stupid for telling her all my business about Q ass.

"It's ok Jemima. I was just calling you to tell you that Tierra was killed last night," she sobbed into the phone.

"Please tell me that this is a joke, not my best friend," I cried out, dropping the phone as I fell to the floor.

Londyn

This couldn't be real. I just spoke to her last night from the car when I was stalking Q's ass and she told me to leave and come chill with her. I regret not listening to her because maybe she would still be here right now. Out of nowhere, I got a burst of energy as I ran out of the house to get to my best friend house because I knew this had to be a sick joke. The tears blurred my vision, but I was determined to make it to her house just for her to jump out of the closet, screaming that she got me. She was always the jokester out of all of us, so it wouldn't be the first time and I'm praying that it's wasn't her last time. She never involved her mother before so that was the only thing that had me thinking that it might be some truth to her being dead.

When I pulled up to her block, I knew that it was true, the hood was out, and somebody already had candles lit around a poster board with her picture. I got out of the car to a million *I'm sorry about your friend* that followed with hugs. I didn't want anything from anybody if they couldn't bring my friend back. I finally made it into the building, getting on the elevator. When I got off on her floor, my heart sunk knowing that she wouldn't be answering the door for me ever again. Her mother pulled me into her arms as soon as she saw me because I broke down as soon as that door opened.

Giving My Heart to A Gangsta

My heart stopped momentarily when I heard her father tell a dude that I never met before that they found her in her mother's car. Her throat was sliced, along with her windows being broken out and all her tires slashed; it took me back to what Q said to me earlier. I know what I was thinking but was Q really that fucked up of a person to take someone's life because he was pissed about his fucking car? I swear, if he had anything to do with doing this to my best friend, his ass was going to pay. I wasn't going to say anything to the family about what I was thinking because her father is some gangsta nigga that wasn't in her life.

He probably would have killed Q on some guilt shit, avenging her death being he hasn't been shit but a damn dead-beat ass father.

I stayed at Tierra's house for about another hour before leaving because it was becoming overwhelming watching everyone else breakdown. When I got back to my car, I called Q, but he sent my call straight to voicemail, pissing me off. I drove to a few of the spots that I knew he frequent but didn't see him, so I decided to go back to my house until I pulled up to the red light and spotted his navigator parked. I only noticed that it was his truck because of his personalized license plate so when the light changed, I pulled up beside it to see if anyone was inside. Seeing no one inside, I backed up and parked my car behind his truck, trying to figure out which one of the stores on the strip that he might have been in. I didn't have to wait long before he was coming out of the Jamaican restaurant with that same bitch in tow from the club. I jumped out of the car so fast not caring that he bust my shit earlier for 'disrespecting him' as he called it.

"Q, you don't see me ringing your fucking phone?" I barked, walking up on him.

"This bitch here," I heard him say.

"Oh, so now I'm a bitch. I wasn't a bitch when you just had your head between my fucking legs. Now listen, I don't give a fuck what you got going on with this bitch, I just need to talk to you now," I demanded just as Malik and Nicola's hoe ass exited the restaurant.

"Go get in the truck. I'll just be a minute," he told the bitch, handing her the keys.

He grabbed me by my arm, pulling me towards the corner of the block before going off on me, but I didn't give a shit.

"I don't know what your fucking problem is Jemima but I'm sick of you with this bullshit. Stop playing with me before you force me to put a bullet in your fucking head," he growled before pushing me against the building wall we were standing in front of.

"Did you kill Tierra?" I yelled, not giving a fuck about his threats.

"Fuck that bitch and fuck you too," he said and all I saw was red when I attacked his ass.

I tried to take his fucking head off as I punched and kept punching with him trying to get control of my hands. When I dug my fingernails in his eyes, that's when he pushed me so hard I went flying, hitting the ground hard and bumping my head in the process of the fall. He was walking towards me with his pistol out and I feared for my life until I saw Malik come and talk him down and away from me. I felt so much hatred towards him in that moment and I knew if I had been carrying a gun, his ass would have been dead.

When I picked myself up off the ground, I felt dizzy as if I was going to fall back to the ground as I balanced myself up against the building.

"Hey, are you ok?" I heard someone ask.

When I looked up, I saw this nice-looking guy that looked like he was about 6'3 the way he was now towering over me. He was a coffee with cream complexion, brown eyes that made me believe that I could trust him considering I wasn't feeling the opposite sex right now. He had me in a deeper daze then the one I was in from hitting my head on the ground.

"I'm ok," I finally spoke.

I was disoriented for a few seconds, but I felt better to walk to my car and take my ass home where I should have gone instead of looking for Q.

"Are you sure because you hit your head pretty hard?" He said, letting me know that he saw what happened.

I was now embarrassed that he saw how Q treated me, so I really wanted to get to my car and away from him. I attempted to walk to my car and once again, I almost fell but he caught me and helped me over to a black expedition and I started to panic. I started thinking that maybe he was a friend of Q's pretending to look out for me so that he could take me somewhere to kill me. If he was really concerned, why the hell did he watch what was going on and not intervene when I really needed his help.

"Shorty, I'm not trying to hurt you. I'm just trying to make sure that you get home safe because you can't drive like this," he said once I hesitated to get in his truck.

"I can't just leave my car," I told him.

192

Giving My Heart to A Gangsta

"If you let me take you home, I promise that once you're straight you can call me, and I'll take you back to pick up your car," he promised. So, I got into his truck to let him drive me home.

When he pulled up to my building, he helped me out of the truck and inside, giving me his number before turning to leave.

"Hey, you didn't tell me your name," I reminded him even though I never told him my name either.

"You were acting like I was going to take you somewhere and murder your ass, so it slipped my mind," he chuckled, showing off some cute ass dimples.

"I'm sorry I really didn't mean to treat you like that. I was just scared after what happened," I admitted. "My name is Jemima."

"My name is Ahmad. You be sure to take care of that bump on your head and give me a call when you're ready for me to take you to get your car," he said before walking towards the elevator.

I wished that my mother was still alive because it was times like these when I needed her the most. *I can really say that I have no one now that Tierra is gone too*, I thought as I went into the bathroom to take a shower.

Chapter Twenty
(Katrina)

Shit has been crazy this past week and it was taking its toll on me. I wasn't bothered at first that Q was blowing me up until he stopped. It was going on over a week now and I've heard nothing from him. Now I was blowing him up, but he wasn't answering. I was sick of playing phone tag with his ass. My mom and I went to the old building to give our condolences to Tierra's mom and I swear that I'm so happy to be out of the neighborhood. I was hoping to see Q ass in the neighborhood so that was the real reason I even went. I couldn't stand Tierra's ass before she died. I mean, I wouldn't have wished death on her in that manner being they found out that she was pregnant at the time she was killed. My mom went to the funeral, but I opted out of going being I felt that paying my respect at the home was enough for me.

I just got out of school, so I was waiting on Tamika to come out so that we could ride home together. After waiting fifteen minutes, I called her. Our relationship still wasn't the same being she wanted me to bite my tongue on that bullshit

194

that happened at her house. I couldn't bite my tongue because I didn't want my best friend in no casket or the reason that another person ended up in a casket. She was still seeing Aaron, but I have no idea if she was still creeping with Malik or not. If she was, she wasn't going to tell me.

When she answered the call, she said that she left with Aaron. That's the shit I was talking about. She still acting funny style but it's all good. I called Q's phone to see if he was finally going to take my call just for him to send me to voicemail. So, I got in my car and headed to his house.

As soon as I pulled up, I felt butterflies in my stomach as nervousness started to set in being I wasn't trying to have a replay of what happened at Jemima's apartment. *I mean, he wasn't fucking with me anymore, so he had to be fucking with someone,* I thought while getting out of the car. I knocked on the door and waited until he opened the door. When he did, he had my ass in a daze. He was standing at the door with no shirt on and some gray sweats that had his afternoon wood on display, causing my temperature to rise.

"What are you doing here?" He asked coldly like he didn't miss me at all.

Londyn

"I came here because you weren't answering any of my calls," I said to him and he chuckled.

"So, you ignore all my calls but get in your feeling when I decided to do the same thing to your ass. Yo, check this out. I don't have time for these kiddy ass games you been playing not acting your fucking age. I been dealing with the shit because a nigga was feeling you and wanted to be with you, but you got a nigga fucked up if you think I'm going to keep chasing behind your ass for some shit that has nothing to do with me. Tamika going on with her relationship with Aaron without a care in the world while you out here advocating for her and fucked up yours."

I knew he was right, but he didn't have to talk to me the way he was talking to me and I swear something about him seemed different. The fact that he still had me standing outside of the door proved that he wasn't feeling me anymore, not fucking with me or both.

"So, do we have to have this conversation on your front porch?" I asked him because he had yet to invite me inside.

When he let me inside, I watched as he picked up his phone and told some female that he was facetiming with that he would hit her back in a few.

Giving My Heart to A Gangsta

"Who was that? The last time I checked, we were still together," I questioned.

"Still together? So, if that was true, why the fuck was you ignoring my calls?" He barked.

"I wasn't ready to talk to you. That's why I didn't answer your calls," I admitted.

"Ok, and I wasn't ready to talk to your ass so why the fuck you show up to my door?"

"Why are you handling me like this, Q?"

"Listen, I know you think that the sun rises and sets on your ass, but I'm done kissing it. If you want to be childish, you need to go fuck with one of those young niggas at your school. I'm a grown ass man that don't have time for this juvenile shit you be on."

"So, you're breaking up with me?" I asked on the verge of tears.

"I don't know what I'm doing right now but what I do know is I'm not doing this bullshit with you anymore. If you have an issue with me then handle that shit as you see fit, but don't blame me for some shit another nigga doing."

"I'm sorry," I apologized just as his phone rang.

Londyn

I could see that it was a facetime call from the same chick so when he walked out of the room, my feelings were hurt. I wanted to just walk out and say fuck it, but I didn't because that would have been childish, especially if I was trying to see if we were still going to be together.

I wasn't too sure because the way he used to look at me was gone and replaced with a look as if he could care less if I wanted to be with him or not. I didn't mean to push him away. I was just trying to get him to understand that Malik was wrong so when he wasn't trying to hear me, it pissed me off. He came back into the room with a wide ass smile on his face and I knew that he was feeling that chick the same way he started off feeling me.

"So, that's what we doing now, Q? You're just going to disrespect me in my face taking that call from a female like I'm not here."

"Why do I have to respect your feelings when you didn't respect mine? This is not a one-way street, shorty. You need to treat me the same way you want to be treated. I didn't do shit to you and treated you like a fucking queen, so like I said, miss me with all the extra bullshit. If you want to be with a nigga, it's time that you start showing that shit or I'm gone."

Giving My Heart to A Gangsta

"I want to be with you, Q, but my question to you is why would you start something with someone else? If we're going to be together, are you going to leave all communication alone with whoever she is?" I needed to know.

"I met shorty at the club. She doesn't live here. She was just visiting," he responded like that answered my question.

It's a lot you could do on a facetime call that would equal to cheating so I was going to need him to dead the shit. I didn't want to argue or fuss with him anymore because I didn't want us to be on the outs again, so I just let it go for now. I told him that I was going to call so that we could talk more later because I needed to get home and do homework. I needed to make things right with Tamika too. I didn't know if he was going to hit the female up again, but I didn't have time to worry about it right now, so I just kissed him and told him again that I would call him.

I sat in my car for a few minutes not really feeling confident that Q and I were going to be ok due to the vibe that I got from him. If he had any plans on making things right between us. Whether I answered his calls or not, he would not have been entertaining the next female. I called Tamika to let her know that I was on my way home and would be stopping by so that we could talk. I needed my best friend back because we never went this long without talking on a best friend level. I needed to talk to her about how this nigga Q was acting. I needed some advice from her because I didn't know what to think about his actions. When I got home, Aaron was leaving her house, so I said what's up to him before going inside to get my damn friend back.

She was sitting on the couch with her English workbook on her lap. I went and sat next to her on the couch, so I could get it over with.

"Are you ready to tell me why you're acting funny style towards me? I have always been outspoken and never sugarcoated anything, so what's the problem now?" I asked her.

"I'm not acting funny style, Katrina and I would never ask you not to be who you are, but I will ask that you not kick me when I'm already down. Everything that you said to me was true and I knew that it was true, but I was already feeling like a damn fool. I felt that you just came hard disregarding what I was feeling in that moment. I love you and nothing will ever change that, but I need for you to understand that sometimes I just need you to say you fucked up but it's going to be alright in that moment. Now, had you come the next day and told me how much of a damn fool I was, I would have listened wholeheartedly, but in that moment, I didn't want to hear it."

"I was caught up in the moment same as you and most of what came out of my mouth was from fear of something happening to you. I meant everything that I said to you but you're right, I could have saved the lecture for another day once I saw that Q's uncle had it under control. With that being said, I'm sorry and I just want my friend back because I have mad shit to talk to you about like right now," I told her.

"I accept your apology now give me the tea." We laughed.

"So, I got into it with Q because he wasn't trying to hear me when I was talking about his friend, so I stop taking his calls. After a while, he stopped calling and I wasn't sweating it until I hadn't spoken to him in like a week. I started blowing up his phone, but he wasn't answering me, pissing me off. Afterschool today, I showed up to his place and when he let me in, he was talking to some female on facetime. His vibe wasn't the same vibe that he always had towards me; he was acting like he didn't want to fuck with me anymore. He basically called me childish and told me that he's a grown man and maybe I need to be checking for those young niggas at our school. In the middle of me apologizing to him, the bitch facetimed him again and he left out of the room to talk to her like I wasn't still in the house. I asked about her and he just said that she was someone that he met at the club, but she doesn't live here. He never said that he wasn't going to talk to her again. He agreed that we will still be in a relationship, but his body language said something else to me."

"Katrina, you might have pushed him away," she said the same thing that I was thinking.

"I don't understand how I pushed him away not talking to him for a few days, it wasn't like I was never going to speak to him again."

"I know that, but this is the second time that you stopped speaking to him about something that had nothing to do with him. Had you answered his call, he probably wouldn't have even gone to the club that night and some bitch wouldn't already have his nose open. She doesn't live here so I suggest that you do everything in your power to get his nose open the way it was when he bought you that damn phone, car and house that you're living in. Shit, you and his ass were practically married if you ask me behind all the shit he's done for you already," she laughed.

Now I was thinking that maybe I should have stayed at his house and really made up with some make up sex. He probably got right back on the phone with her as soon as I left being he knew that I wouldn't know one way or the other, I thought as I told Tamika I would call her later.

Chapter Twenty-One
(Quentin)

I just got out of the shower and soon as I was finished getting dressed, Malik was ringing my damn phone. I hope he wasn't calling about no street shit because I had some shit of my own to handle today and didn't have time for no bullshit.

"What's up?" I answered.

"Yo, nigga, what the fuck did you do to that girl, Londyn? She got Nicola blowing my shit up telling me to tell you to holla at her," Malik clowned.

"Nah, I can't fuck with her no more. Me and my shorty got back together, and she laid down the law," I laughed.

Katrina came back to my house that night and fucked me like she's been fucking all her life and not just for a month. She had a nigga tap out and after my ass tapped out, she made me erase every social existence that I had on Londyn's ass. I'm not going lie and say I wasn't feeling shorty because I was, but she lived in Georgia, so it wasn't like we could be together. I wasn't with no long-distance relationship but if Katrina didn't get her shit together, I probably would have tried it knowing I would have still been hitting local pussy.

"Say word nigga," he laughed.

"Nigga, word. She wasn't playing with my ass knowing exactly what to do to get my ass to do whatever she wanted. So, tell your chick to tell her cousin that I will not be contacting her again, but I enjoyed our time together."

"You a cold ass nigga. You could've at least called her and let her know what was up before blocking her ass."

"Just let Nicola know what's up so that she could tell her cousin. Now get off my line. I got shit to handle," I told him.

"Call me if you need me," he said, already knowing where I was going.

Malik was the only one of my friends that knew that my parents weren't dead because he was the only nigga that I trusted. My uncle raised me from the time I was a year old since my father was incarcerated for trying to kill my mother. He didn't kill her, but he messed her up for life to where her mind is gone to the point where she wasn't able to take care of me. At the time I was born, my grandparents were all deceased on my mom and dad side of the family. Since my mom didn't have any other siblings, my uncle took me. When I was old enough, he explained to me the circumstances of what happened between my parents. So, I understood why he would take me to visit my mom but not my dad. Once I was old enough to visit on my own, I made sure to see her at least once a month. After every visit, it always broke me down to see her like that. Her mind comes and goes to the point that she makes me think that she knows who I am just to fade out making me think otherwise.

Sometimes I get discouraged, but it doesn't stop me from going to see her because I'm all she got, so I wasn't giving up on her. I moved her to a better establishment about a year ago and these doctors are optimistic that the new medication that she's on will help her restore memories. I don't know why my uncle had her in the place she was in for so long because she wasn't getting the care that she needed. Had he put her where I have her now, she probably would have gained her memory back years ago. It wasn't like he didn't have the money to afford this place back then.

I arrived at the Rehabilitation center and sat in my car for a few minutes preparing myself mentally before going inside. I be wanting to breakdown and cry when I be seeing her sometimes; that's the reason I always come alone. I walked inside and was greeted by Ms. Emma at the front desk who was wearing a big smile on her face.

"How are you, Quentin? It's good to see you again," she smiled.

Ms. Emma was an older woman, but I swear she be flirting with me on the low, showing all her fake teeth, acting all giddy and shit.

"I'm doing ok, Ms. Emma, now that I got to see that pretty smile of yours," I told her.

After signing in, I went to leave to go to my mother's room but not before looking back and seeing Ms. Emma fanning herself with the sign in sheet. She had me cracking up to myself knowing her ass was too old to be flirting with my young ass. I took a deep breath before walking into my mother's room preparing for the worst, but to my surprise, she was up sitting near the window looking out. Her hair wasn't sitting on top of her head like always being she never allowed anyone to touch it. She was wearing her hair up in a high ponytail with a blue ribbon that matched the blue dress with yellow flowers she was wearing. I walked over and took a seat just watching her as she continued to look out of the window, not acknowledging that I even walked into the room. She seemed to be in good spirits as I caught her smiling a few times at whatever was going on in that head of hers.

"This is wrong. We need to tell him," I heard my mom say just above a whisper.

"Mom, are you talking to me?" I questioned but she just continued talking out her head.

"Vick hurt me, Vick hurt me," she repeated as she started rocking back and forth. "I'm so sorry," she whispered as she continued to rock, closing her eyes as the tears fell.

I walked over to her to wipe the tears from her eyes and she pulled me in hugging me tight; something she hasn't done in a long time. I hugged her back and I swear she made me feel safe in her arms. So safe that she had a thug shedding tears.

"Quentin, my baby," she sobbed into my ear before letting me go at the sound of someone entering the room.

"Hello, Mr. McKenzie. Good to see you again," he greeted with a handshake.

"How are you Dr. Quam."

"I'm good and like I said, it's good to see you because I was just going to call you to come in so that I could speak with you. So, if you could just come with me to my office, I'll try to make it as quick as possible so that you could continue your visit," he said so I followed him out.

"You can have a seat," he said before walking around and taking a seat at his desk.

"Your mom has been showing progress since we started her on the new medication which is a good thing. Some things are clear to me, but I have to tell you that some of her accounts have been troubling," he informed.

"What do you mean?" I asked him, not quite following what he was trying to say.

"Last week, your mom was asking for her husband which confused me, being her records stated that her husband was responsible for the blunt force trauma that caused her condition. So, the day after that, she kept insisting that someone named Vick hurt her. When I began questioning how he hurt her, she got frustrated. Before she completely shut down, she went into a bag that's been in her belongings since she arrived here and handed me these photos," he said, going into the folder on his desk and handing me the pictures.

I took the pictures from him and the first picture was a pic of a newborn baby boy who I'm assuming to be me. The next one was my mother in a picture embracing my uncle in a hug at what looked to be a jail pic. I didn't even know that he spent time in jail because he never mentioned it to me. What bothered me about the picture was that she looked to be like nine months pregnant in the picture. There were a few more jail pictures but I didn't see my dad in any of the other pictures, so my mind was spinning with thoughts of my own. I told the doctor that I didn't know what the photos meant or what my mom was trying to tell him, until I thought back to what she was saying in the room. I thought back to the day that my uncle told me how my mother was able to call 911 after being attacked and how she told the emergency dispatcher that her husband hurt her when asked. The wheels in my head were spinning as I thought about the movie the Fugitive when Harrison Ford was accused of killing his wife because of something she said to the emergency dispatcher. It was only one way to find out if what I was thinking was the case. And if it was, I swear on everything I love, my uncle is going to feel my wrath.

After getting everything squared away with the doctor, I went to my mom's room to kiss her bye and to tell her that I would see her soon. I called up my uncle to put my plan in motion just to see where this nigga's head was at and if he was going to take the bait.

Giving My Heart to A Gangsta

"Hey unc, are you busy?" I asked him as soon as he answered the call.

"Nah, what's up?"

"Do you remember when I told you that the doctor was going to start my mom on a new medication?"

"Barely. What's up?" He asked like he was getting impatient with me.

"Well, it seems to be working because today she actually remembered who I was and called me by my name. She called me her baby, even asking for my father. The doctor mentioned that she was trying to tell him who hurt her even though we already know that it was my father. The doctor informed me that with this new medication, it isn't going to be long before she starts getting her memory back," I lied, praying I wasn't laying it on too thick.

"That's good news Q and I'm happy that you got to experience that with her today being that's what you wanted for a long time now. Are you still there?" He asked me.

"No, I left because she was falling asleep, so I told her that I would be back to see her soon now that she's starting to remember things. But let me get off this phone so that I could get to Katrina's crib because she's been blowing me up all day," I lied again.

"Ok, I'll holla at you later," he said before ending the call.

I drove away from the rehabilitation center and parked my truck a few blocks away. I waited, praying that I was wrong about what I was thinking. I called Katrina up to let her know that I needed for her to tell her mother that if my uncle called and asked if I was there with her for her to say that I was. I told her that I would explain later but I wasn't going to tell her the truth, but I would tell her something. She said that she would do it. After getting off the phone with her, it was time to play the waiting game and pray that the call never came.

I didn't even realize that I had dozed off until the ringing of my phone woke me up and when I saw that it was Ms. Emma calling, I answered. She let me know that my uncle just left from trying to visit with my mother and she told him exactly what I told her to tell him. I told her that I was going to have something nice for her when I come back to visit before ending the call pissed off. All this fucking time I was being loyal to a fucking snake ass nigga that pretended to give a fuck about me. He didn't give a fuck about me because if he did, the best thing his bitch ass could have done was allow the state to take my ass after the shit he done.

Chapter Twenty-Two
(Uncle Vick)

"Fuck!" I cursed, leaving out of the rehabilitation center.

That fat bitch at the desk informed me that visiting hours were over ten minutes ago and as much as I tried to bribe her ass to let me see Carla, she refused. I wanted to snatch that big mama's house wig right off her fucking head, but I knew that I probably would have had to drop the security guard. The bitch had the nerve to be all up in my business, asking me my relation to Carla like she didn't just tell me that visiting hours were over. So, when she said that visiting hours started at ten tomorrow, I told her that's when she could be all up in my business. The last thing I needed right now was for Carla to start remembering shit. Had she listened to me back then, none of this shit would have happened. She would be home to raise Q with my brother living happily ever after. Instead, she's here and barely has a relationship with her son.

My brother was working late the evening that everything happened. That night, I stopped by to see Q like I always did whenever he wasn't home. I was sitting in the living room with

Londyn

Q on my lap when Carla came and sat on the sofa saying that she needed to talk to me. I thought she was going to question me about the rumor that were floating around about me getting one of her friends pregnant. When she told me that she wanted to tell my brother Lester, that he wasn't Q's father, I tried to talk her out of it. She just went on and on about how it was wrong to allow him to raise a son that wasn't his and how it wasn't fair that I was only allowed to see my son whenever he wasn't home. I tried to convince her that she was going to hurt him by telling him some shit like that, but she wasn't trying to hear me, saying she couldn't live with the guilt anymore. When she said that she asked God for forgiveness and I needed to do the same, I knew there was no getting through to her because she had already made up her mind. I knew that if she told Lester that we'd been messing around for years and Q was my son, God wouldn't ever be able to save us. Lester wouldn't have hesitated to kill the both of us. He was big on loyalty and if you crossed him, it wouldn't matter to him if you were family or not. After I put Q to bed that night, I tried to reason with her one more time and she still wouldn't budge so she left me no choice. I took the cast iron frying pan off the stove, hitting her from behind. I didn't stop hitting her until she was no longer moving. I left out of the house unaware that she wasn't dead and found the strength to pull the phone down and dial 911. When the dispatcher asked her who attacked her, she said his name. So, Lester was arrested for attempted murder. He fucked up his alibi because he was in fact working late that night but got off early. Instead of going home, which would have prevented what happened at the house, he went to the bar. No one at the bar could remember him being there that night. He had no proof that he wasn't at home attempting to kill his wife. So, he was convicted of attempted murder. Listening to the recording of the 911 call in court, I knew that Carla disregarded the question and was calling out for my brother, not naming him as the person who attacked her. But, they didn't know that, and she couldn't tell them different.

I raised Q as my nephew, never telling him that he was my son because that was a secret that I planned on taking to my grave. I had to make sure that Carla takes her last breath tomorrow. I promise that I will not be botching the job this time because I be damned if anyone will know the truth of my disloyalty to my brother.

I stopped by the Chinese restaurant to get something to eat before heading home because I had no plans on cooking anything. I had a lot on my mind so after eating, I was going to shower and go to bed so that I could get up early to get to the rehabilitation center at ten. I wanted to be there early to smother her ass with a pillow, leaving her looking as if she was sleeping peacefully.

Once I made it home, I sat my bag down on the counter before going into my room to change out of my clothes to get comfortable before eating.

"What's up, unc?" Q said from behind me, scaring the shit out of me.

"Nigga, don't be sneaking around my shit. Make some fucking noise to let a nigga know you up in my shit," I barked, walking towards the kitchen.

"My bad, unc. What's good with you?" He asked me.

"I'm good. I just ran out to get something to eat. Do you want some Chinese food?" I asked him.

"Nah, I already ate. I just came by to holla at you about something."

"Cool, give me a minute," I told him, fixing my plate and grabbing a beer from the fridge before joining him in the living room.

"What's up? Talk to me," I told him taking a swig from my beer.

Giving My Heart to A Gangsta

"What happened the night that my mother was attacked? I mean, you never really went into details about what happened that night," he asked, causing me to choke as the beer went down the wrong pipe.

"I told you what happened that night, Q, from what I was told by the police that investigated the case. I wasn't there so I wouldn't have any details of what took place before or after the attack," I lied after I stopped coughing.

"So, you weren't there that night?" He asked, sounding like he was accusing me of something.

"Nigga, say what the fuck you trying to say and stop with that beating around the bush bullshit. Get the shit off your chest."

"I just want the fucking truth unc. Or should I start calling you pops?"

"Listen, I don't know what your mother said to you but I'm sure whatever it was she was just talking out of her head like she always does," I tried to convince him.

"Don't worry about what my mom said or what she didn't say. I need you to fucking explain these pictures to me," he said, throwing the pictures down on the coffee table.

Londyn

I didn't really need to pick up the pictures because I already knew what pictures he was referring to. I was just going to keep my cool because those pictures didn't mean shit and could be just as innocent as his mom visiting me. I picked the pictures up just to appease him before answering him and hoped that he left the shit alone once I explained.

"I got caught up on a violation and had to do six months in jail. Your mom came to visit me a few times. We were all cool back then and when your father couldn't make it, he would send her. That's all it was to those pictures," I lied with a straight face.

"So, you going to sit here and lie to my fucking face, nigga? My mother told me that you were the one that hurt her that night so I'm going to ask you one more time to keep the shit real with me," he demanded.

"Q, you're not about to disrespect me in my shit so I need for you to get the fuck out and come back when you're ready to be respectful. I raised your little fucking ass when I could have easily let the state take your ass, so be thankful nigga."

"So, you think I'm fucking playing with you? Do this look like I'm playing with your ass?" He barked, now pointing a gun at me.

Giving My Heart to A Gangsta

I wasn't bothered by him pointing his gun at me because I knew that he wasn't going to do shit to me. He was hurt and wanted answers. Answers that I didn't want to give him because he wouldn't understand. All that should matter to his ass is that I took him in and treated him like a little king not wanting for shit. I guess that would have been too much to ask for. This is how his ass decides to repay me; by pointing a gun in my fucking face.

"Q, put the fucking gun down and stop disrespecting me in my fucking house. You were a kid. You wouldn't understand what happened between grown folks so don't even try. I told you that I had nothing to do with what happened to your mother and that I wasn't even there the night the shit went down."

"Arrgh!" I screamed out as he shot me in my knee. "Are you fucking crazy?" I went to grab at him but fell from the pain shooting through my knee.

"I'm not crazy but I do know that I'm not fucking playing with you, nigga. I want the truth, so get to talking, bitch," he barked and the look in his eyes told me that he wasn't fucking around.

Londyn

"Q, your mother and I were in love when we started messing around and she got pregnant, but I promise you that I wasn't there the night the shit went down," I told him.

"Fuck!" I screamed again as he shot me in my other knee.

"I swear I will kill you dead and not give a fuck if you don't stop lying to me," he threatened.

I was in excruciating pain, so I couldn't even get close to the coffee table to pull the drawer open to get my gun. He was my son, but this nigga shot me twice. So if I got ahold of my gun, I wasn't going to hesitate to put two bullets in his fucking chest. I had blood leaking all over my fucking floor and his ass just stood there like he never gave a fuck about the man that raised his ass and always made sure that he was straight. I knew if I told him the truth he wasn't going to spare my life, so I needed to buy some time and try to get to my gun.

"Q, I'm losing a lot of blood. If you ever gave a fuck about me, go get something to stop the blood and I promise you I will tell you the truth," I tried.

"You must think that I'm a stupid nigga. You must have forgot what you just said about you raising me. I know you better than you know yourself, nigga. Now speak, because the next bullet is going in your fucking head."

Giving My Heart to A Gangsta

"Q, I loved your mother, but I respected the fact that she was with my brother, so I never forced her to make a choice. When she got pregnant with you and told me that it was my child, we agreed that we weren't going to say anything to anyone. I was good with being in your life as your uncle because I was wrong for even sleeping with my brother's wife. Your mother started feeling a way about lying to your father about him raising a child that wasn't his and the fact that I only got to spend time with you as my son when he wasn't around. She called me over that night to tell me that she was going to tell him the truth. I begged and pleaded with her not to say anything to him, but she wouldn't listen. I told her that if she told him that he would kill us both, but she started talking about how she already asked God for forgiveness, so she was going to tell him. I had no choice. I picked up the cast iron frying pan and hit her with it until she wasn't moving anymore," I told him.

I saw the hurt in his eyes as he pulled the trigger, hitting me in my chest twice, not caring that I was begging for my life. I heard him tell someone to burn this bitch down before he raised the gun, shooting me in the head.

Chapter Twenty-Three
(Katrina)

When I made it to Q's house, I was nervous. I didn't know what to say to him after losing his uncle because my mom was a mess. He has been standoffish since the funeral and hasn't been himself, so I came to see if he was doing ok. He opened the door laughing hard as hell like someone just told the funniest joke and that's when I realized that he had fucking company. This nigga didn't seem like he was mourning or how he sounded on the phone earlier, so I was confused because he told me that he just wanted to be alone.

"Do you have company?" I asked with attitude evident in my voice.

"Yeah, Malik stopped by so we just chilling," he laughed.

His eyes were low, and his voice was slurred. I knew that he was smoking and drinking, so it was pissing me off.

"Q, what are you doing?" I heard from inside.

"That doesn't sound like Malik, Q." I pushed passed him going inside.

Giving My Heart to A Gangsta

I walked inside seeing Malik on the couch hugged up with Nicola hoe ass and some bitch sitting across from them.

"What the fuck is going on here, Q? When I spoke to you, I could have sworn you said you needed to be alone," I said to him.

"So, if he said he needed to be alone, why are you here?" The bitch sitting on the sofa said and they all laughed.

"So, I'm a fucking joke to you Q?"

"Katrina, chill. They just came by to check on a nigga. Come to the back and let me holla at you," he said, pulling me towards the room, causing the bitch to mouth off.

I was trying hard to ignore the bitch, but I was a few seconds from taking her fucking head off right along with Q's fucking head.

"Listen, I understand that you just lost your uncle but don't think that I'm going to allow you to disrespect me. I'm supposed to be your girlfriend, and you tell me that you need some time alone but invite over the same bitch that I had you block. I'm going to give you the chance to tell that bitch that she has to go before I drag her ass up out of here," I barked.

Londyn

He left out of the room with me right behind him because I meant what I said and had no problem dragging both those bitches up out of here.

"Nicola, it's time for you and Londyn to bounce," he told them.

"Word, it's like that when I drove all this way to see you?!" Londyn yelled.

"Shorty, I didn't ask you to do no stupid shit like that when I wasn't even fucking with your ass no more."

"I swear you're a lame," she said, getting up and grabbing her shit.

"He can't be too much of a lame being your thirsty ass just admitted to driving all the way here to see about a nigga that played your ass to the left," I instigated.

"Londyn, come on. Let's just go," Nicola told her, giving her some good advice because she didn't want to go there with me.

Malik's ass was high as shit because he sat on the couch thinking that everything was funny instead of getting his bitch up out of here. The bitch Londyn had one more thing to say and I was going to mop her ass with the floor; I wasn't playing.

Giving My Heart to A Gangsta

Q was about to get punched in his throat too for letting the bitch inside after we just discussed this bitch.

"Fuck, you Q and fuck this bit…"

That's all she got out of her mouth before I grabbed her by her ugly ass braids and swung her ass to the floor. She grabbed my shirt and pulled me down with her, but that didn't stop me from pounding her fucking face. She pulled my hair, trying to wrap her hands around my braids and I lost it. I wasn't trying to get no bald spot in my shit or have this bitch pull my edges out.

"Get off me, Malik. I'm not going to stand here and let that bitch fuck my cousin up," I heard Nicola say.

Her cousin wouldn't be getting fucked up right now if she didn't take her time getting the bitch up out of here thinking shit was sweet. Q finally got Londyn's hands from around my hair and grabbed me in a bear hug, but I was still holding on to her ass and she was being dragged as he pulled me away.

"Katrina, let her go now," he demanded.

I let the bitch go because I already fucked her up, so I was satisfied with shutting her the hell up. Now I was telling him to get the fuck off me. I swear until I met Q's ass I have never had to fight a bitch before. I know that I said that I was tired of it,

225

but it felt good putting these bitches in their place. Malik opened the door and closed it back fast, telling Q that the police were out front. My ass started panicking, praying this bitch didn't want to press charges.

"Listen, everybody go sit the fuck down and act like nothing fucking happened," he barked.

"Malik, get all that shit up off the table," he told him.

"Fuck sitting down. I'm pressing charges against this bitch," Londyn cried.

"If you say anything to the fucking cops, bitch, you better pray they put your fucking ass in protective custody." Q threatened.

The knock came on the door the only way the fucking police knew how to knock, causing me to jump even though I knew who it was. Q's ass was looking nervous like he was guilty of some shit walking to the door to open it. I tried to fix my hair quick so that they wouldn't get suspicious if they did enter the home. I prayed they didn't because Londyn's face was fucked up.

"What can I do for you officers?" Q asked.

Giving My Heart to A Gangsta

"Are you Quentin McKenzie?" One of the officers asked him.

He hesitated, and I started getting nervous. If one of the neighbors called about a noise complaint, do they come being so formal?

"Yes, I'm Quentin, but what is this about?"

"Quentin McKenzie, we have a warrant for your arrest for the assault on Jemima Garrett," the officer answered before reading him his rights.

"This is some bullshit. I never assaulted anyone," Q barked.

Once they put the handcuffs on him, my tears fell because I was pissed. I didn't believe that he put his hands on that damn girl. Malik was going off, but it fell on deaf ears as they hauled Q off to the awaiting police car. I let those two bitches know that they needed to leave because I was going to lock up his place and head over to the police station with Malik. I asked Malik if it was true that Q assaulted her, and he said that they had words, but he didn't put his hands on her. I didn't believe him because when he said it, he didn't look me in my face and it seemed as if he was hiding something. I wanted to believe that he didn't put his hands on her. He was convincing when he said that he would never put his hands on any woman, but now I wasn't too sure. After locking up his place, I got into my car and followed Malik to the police station, praying that they gave him a desk appearance so that he could be released from their custody.

Malik and I were at the police station for over an hour. No one had come out to speak to us yet and it was pissing me off. I called my mother to let her know that I was at the police station, but she didn't answer so I left her a message letting her know. I didn't expect her to answer the phone because, like I said, she took Vick's death hard. More so because his wife didn't allow her to come to the funeral. She was hurt that she didn't get to say goodbye to him so that was eating her up inside and she was hitting the bottle hard these last few days.

Another hour later, a detective finally came out to speak to us and let us know that Q's name came up in a case that they were investigating so he wouldn't be released anytime soon. He gave us his card and took my number in return, telling me that he would give me a call with an update within the hour. I was confused as to what the hell was going on but talking to Malik ass gave me the impression that he knew something. He wasn't talking so all I could do was go home and wait on the detective to call. Hopefully, Q would use his phone call to call me to let me know what the hell the detective was talking about. I wanted to go to Jemima's place and fuck that bitch up. She's from the hood so she should know that calling the fucking police was a death sentence. Stupid bitch probably called because she's in her feelings about him not wanting to fuck with her ass anymore, but I'm going to see her ass.

When I got home, my mother was passed out in her room, so I called Tamika to let her know what was going on. She seemed to be more interested in Malik's ass, asking stupid questions about him. I had to tell her to focus because it was my man behind bars. After getting off the phone with her, I waited on a call from Q or the detective that never came so I showered and took my ass to bed.

The next morning, I waited downstairs in my car for Tamika so that we could ride to school together but my mind was elsewhere. I wasn't going to go to school, but I still hadn't heard anything from Q. I wasn't going to sit home when I could go to school. I already missed too many days when his uncle passed.

"I don't feel good this morning, girl. I've been throwing up all fucking night," Tamika complained after getting in the car.

Londyn

"Did you bring any crackers with you?" I asked her because they made her feel much better last time.

"Nope, it seems like I can't keep anything down so I'm not trying to eat nothing right now. My mom told me to suck on this ginger candy. I just put them in my bag praying that I could make it through the day. Have you heard anything else about Q?" She asked me.

"No, he didn't call me yet. If I don't hear anything by the time we get out of school, I'm going to call the detective." I told her.

"Did you hear from Malik? He might have called him."

"No, I haven't heard from his ass either. I told you that I think he knows exactly what is going on. Q might have called him and told him not to tell me anything, but I don't know," I stressed, getting a headache with the situation.

"Girl, try not to stress too much. I'm sure that everything will be ok," she tried to assure me.

I wanted to believe that everything was going to be ok, but I wasn't too sure especially after seeing Malik's facial expression when I was questioning him. Q most likely did something stupid and got his ass caught up messing with all these fucking females that had his ass off his game. I knew that

Giving My Heart to A Gangsta

I should have taken my ass home after school, but I just had to do something to get my man out of jail. I was going to pay the bitch, Jemima, a visit and force that bitch to drop the assault charges. I would figure out what to do about whatever case that his name came up on once I get the details. He did so much for me and my mother, so I be damned if I was going to sit back and not try to fix this shit.

I gave myself a pep talk before getting out of the car, reminding myself not to put my hands-on Jemima because I wasn't trying to catch a case too. I took a deep breath before knocking on her door knowing that she was home because her scary ass didn't show up to school today, so I waited for her to answer. She opened the door with a bat in her hand, causing me to chuckle just a bit. Trust, if Q sent someone, she would need more than a damn bat to save her life.

"Listen, I'm just here to talk," I told her.

"What do we possibly have to talk about Katrina? You know just like I know we don't like each other being we're both screwing the same man," she responded but I let that shit slide off my back.

Londyn

She may have been screwing him, but he was my man and she still hasn't come to grips with that fact, so there was no sense arguing about it.

"Can I please come inside so we could talk?" I tried.

"Don't come in here on no bullshit, Katrina. I will not have a problem using this bat," she threatened like it was supposed to scare me.

Chapter Twenty-Four
(Katrina)

I walked into her place and took a seat on the sofa putting my pride to the side ready to beg the bitch to drop the charges against my man.

"So, what do you need to talk to me about?" She asked wearing a smirk on her face knowing damn well what I wanted to talk about.

"Look, I don't know what happened between you and Q but getting him locked up is some bullshit. I know that you don't care for me, but I know you care about him so can you please just drop the charges against him. I know Q and I know that he didn't assault you. He just loss his uncle so this shit is fucked up," I said to her but all she did was laugh making me want to punch her in the face.

"So, I take it that your man hasn't called you and told you anything, being you're sitting here thinking that his ass got locked up for assault. I'm sorry to inform you that your man who walks around like he's God's gift to woman didn't have a problem sleeping with my best friend."

233

Londyn

"What the fuck are you talking about?" I interrupted her because clearly, she was on some bullshit.

"Q was fucking Tierra and she was pregnant by him. He killed her because she wasn't trying to get rid of it. I hope he rots in jail but not before getting fucked in his ass every night so that he will know how it feels to get fucked," she barked angrily.

"Bitch, if you think lying on him is going to make you feel better about him not wanting to be with you, trust me, it's not. I'm sure that he will be released on that bogus shit that you told the police and I pray that he fucks you up for putting him through this bullshit over some dick."

"Trust me when I say that I didn't have to lie about anything of what I just told you. I had no idea that he was screwing my best friend. Her mother showed me all the interactions that he was having with Tierra from her phone messages. So, yes, she was pregnant by him. Yes, he asked her to get rid of it which she declined and yes, he was the last one that saw her the night she was killed. He lured her out of her apartment by telling her that they were going to talk and figure out how they were going to tell us about the baby and that they were going to be together," she teared up.

Giving My Heart to A Gangsta

I felt sick to my stomach and the fact that hurt was written on her face, I had no choice but to believe what she was telling me. It turns out that Q wasn't the man that I thought he was and that shit hurt me to my core knowing that I was ready to do whatever to get him out of jail. It all started to make sense why Tierra kept fucking with me. It had nothing to do with her boyfriend; it was Q's ass the entire time.

"I'm sorry for coming here. I'm going to go," I told her not, knowing what else to say now that her tears were falling and mine were about to fall.

"I think that there is something else you should know because it seems that your friend is just as green to how these hood niggas play. I know that she believes that Malik and Aaron's beef is about her, but it stems from everyone thinking that Aaron was some nerd walking around in these streets. His ass is just as deep in these streets as Malik and Q are. Rumor has it that Aaron's son may very well be Malik's son, but after the girl passed away it was never bought up again. Also, let her know that they both are in this 'whose dick is bigger' type shit going after each other's girlfriend just to prove something. Most likely, Aaron pushed up on Tamika because he knew that she was feeling Malik and Aaron is fucking with Nicola on the low because he knows that she fucks with Malik. The shit is crazy the way they prey on females, but I never thought that it would get my friend killed and Q fighting me like I was a nigga in the street," she sobbed.

I had to get up out of there because this shit was too much to take in right now. And to think, I've had blinders on all this time. I was now sitting in my car with the tears falling from my eyes when my phone rang from a private number. I rejected the call because I knew that it was Q calling. I had questions, but I wasn't ready to talk to him. All he was going to do was lie to me and say that she was telling me lies because he didn't want to be with her. I wasn't buying that bullshit anymore being that she was hurt finding out about him getting her best friend pregnant and killing her because of it. What made his dumb ass not think that they wouldn't look through her phone to see the last call she made or go through her messages? So much for being street smart. I didn't even want to tell Tamika the things that Jemima told me being she was still going hard with Aaron, but I couldn't keep it from her.

When I got home, my mom was in the kitchen cooking. When she looked up at me, the tears fell, and she pulled me into her arms where I cried until I couldn't cry anymore. I told her everything that Jemima told me, and she was in shock the same as I was when I first heard the allegations. She convinced me to call the detective and when I did, he confirmed that Q was being charged for the murder of Tierra, letting me know that he was going to be arraigned sometime tomorrow. After giving me the number to bookings, he ended the call. I sat with the phone to me ear in utter disbelief. I believed that Jemima was telling me what was told to her by Tierra's mother, but in the back of my head, I didn't want to believe it. Hearing the detective confirm it had me having chest pains. This shit was too much to handle right now. My mother tried to get me something to eat but I didn't want to eat. I just went into the bathroom to shower and cried myself to sleep.

The next morning, I woke up to a few missed calls from the private number. I heard my phone ringing I still wouldn't have answered. I wasn't going to school today and I wasn't going to his arraignment even though any other woman probably would have stuck by her man not really knowing if he was guilty or not. I honestly believed that he was. I mean, if they didn't have the messages between him and Tierra, maybe just maybe, I would have believed that maybe someone was fucking with him. But, they had the proof. The text messages didn't prove that he killed her. They only prove that he was the last person to have seen her. I was still stuck on the fact that he was fucking the bitches I was having issues with. Even after he saw how they kept coming for me, he continued to fuck with them. So, that was the reason I wasn't going to show up to his arraignment today. Malik was the one that kept his secret, so he should be the one to ride this shit out with him; not the girlfriend that he deceived time and time again.

My mom was no longer working at Vick's company because his wife, who he never divorced, fired her. She's been looking for work and finally had an interview today. She didn't want to leave me, but I told her that I was going to be fine. She needed this job to get her out of the depressed mood she's been in lately. Tamika has a doctor's appointment today, so I knew that she was going to be home until it was time for her to go. I was going to go and let her know what Jemima shared with me. I didn't want to hurt her, but I needed to let her know. If she found out that I knew, she wouldn't speak to my ass ever again. I called to tell her to unlock the door for me because I was on my way over to speak to her about something.

"Hey, how are you feeling?" I asked her.

"I'm feeling somewhat better today. What's up? Have you heard from Q yet?" She asked me.

"No, I didn't hear from him, but I went to see Jemima yesterday to try and get her to drop the assault charges. She told me that Q didn't have any assault charges and that he was arrested for the murder of Tierra."

"What do you mean the murder of Tierra?" She interrupted.

"Jemima told me that Tierra mother told her about some text messages between Q and Tierra that stated that she was pregnant by him. He was trying to get her to get rid of the baby, but she told him that she wasn't getting rid of the baby. The last text message between them was Q asking her to meet up with him on the night that she was killed, telling her that they were going to talk about the baby. He also told her that they were going to discuss how they were going to tell me and Jemima that they were going to be together and that she was pregnant. I didn't want to believe what she was saying, but she broke down. She was hurt finding out that he was sleeping with her and Tierra," I told her, trying not to tear up.

"Katrina, it's fucked up that he was out there slinging dick but meeting up with her doesn't mean that he killed the bitch. She was grimy, and she proved that by sleeping with Q knowing her bitch ass already had a boyfriend. So, maybe he killed her ass. I'm not defending him but I'm not ready to convict him based on a text message. She may have told him she was going to meet up with him but who's to say that she did. I'm just saying."

"I hear what you're saying but I'm not even in the mindset right now to give him the benefit of the doubt because he played me something crazy. That's not all that she told me, Tamika," I hesitated.

"Well, what else did she have to say?" She asked, waiting.

"She told me that Aaron had beef with Malik before you even started messing with him. According to her, it was rumored that Aaron's son could possibly be Malik's son, but nothing ever came of it being the mother passed away. She said they have been sleeping with each other's girlfriends trying to prove something to each other. Aaron is sleeping with Nicola too just because she's sleeping with Malik. She admitted that she was only telling me because she wanted us to know how grimy these hood niggas are. The only reason Aaron pushed up on you was because he knew that you had a thing for Malik. I don't know how true any of what she told me is true, but I wasn't going to hold on to what she told me without telling you. Oh, and she said that Aaron is in these streets deeper than Q and Malik. But again, I don't know how true it is." I told her, forgetting that part for a minute.

Giving My Heart to A Gangsta

"I'm not tripping off anything that she said until I see the shit for myself. I think that you're a fool not to be there for Q. Never believe something that a trick told your ass and not be there for him like he's been here for you. It may very well be true, but to convict him before hearing him out or finding out if the charges are even going to stick is wrong, Katrina. Her boyfriend could have found out that she was creeping with Q and killed her ass. You see how the fuck Malik ass did me when he found out about Aaron and my baby possibly being his."

"So, do you think that I should go down to the courthouse for his arraignment?" I asked her.

"Katrina, if it was me, I would be there for him until you had facts, just like I'm going to still let Aaron take me to my appointment. When we get back from the appointment, I will be asking him about the things that she said, but I'm not going to just assume that she was telling the truth. I didn't trust those bitches before, so I don't think that I could trust those bitches now."

I heard what she was saying, so I was going to go down to the courthouse for his arraignment to be there for him. No, it didn't mean that I was going to be with him. It just meant that I was going to give his ass the benefit of the doubt and be there for him like he's been here for me. I told her that I was going to go to the courthouse and would call her when I got back home to give her an update.

When I got to the courthouse, Malik was there with his baby mother, so I walked over to him to see if Q was seen or not.

"Hey, did they call his case yet?" I asked him.

"Not yet but his paperwork is in the courtroom, so they should be calling the case soon. He said that he's been trying to reach you," he said but I didn't even respond.

After Q's case was called, I listened intensely as the butterflies danced in my stomach from nervousness. When the judge said that he was releasing him on his own recognizance, I sighed a breath of relief. Everything that I felt or thought before seeing him went out the window because I was praying that he got released. Once in the hallway, he pulled me into him, hugging me tight, thanking me for being here and expressing how he thought I wasn't going to show being I didn't answer any of his calls. I hugged him back still feeling the love that I always felt for him, not caring about nothing in this moment but his being ok.

Giving My Heart to A Gangsta

As soon as we exited the courthouse, him and Malik walked ahead of us talking in hush tones as we followed behind him. They were walking in the opposite direction from where I parked. Before I could get his attention, shots rang out. I knew that I needed to take cover but just like that very day that Q came to my rescue, I stood frozen, praying that he came to save me from being hit. I heard Malik's son's mother scream before falling to the ground and you would think that I would try to get behind a car, but I was so scared that I couldn't move. I heard Q's voice, but I didn't see him because so many people were running for cover. Just as I got my feet to move, I never made it as the bullets invaded my body. I heard Q screaming my name distinctly in the air until I no longer heard anything before everything went black.

Chapter Twenty-Five
(Tamika)

Aaron and I were on our way back from my doctor's appointment and we just arrived on my block when he came to a complete stop. My head had been down playing Words with Friends on my phone, so I turned to look at him, wondering why he hit the brakes so hard. When my eyes followed his and saw that the house that we lived in engulfed in flames, I jumped out of the car just to be stopped. I knew that my mother was at work, but I didn't know if Katrina and her mother was home so panic sunk in as I tried to fight the officer to get to the house. Aaron grabbed me, and I collapsed in his arms, praying that no one was inside the house as my chest heaved up and down as the tears fell from my eyes.

Once the fire was out, we were told that no one was in the home, causing me to thank God. It could have been a bad scene had my friend and her mother been inside. I pulled out my cell phone to call my mother as Aaron spoke to the fire chief. Before I had the chance to call her, my phone was ringing in my hand. It was Q calling me to tell me that Katrina was shot and that I needed to get in touch with her mother and get to the hospital. This had to be a bad fucking dream, but I knew that it was happening because the chest pain that I was feeling was real.

We were all at the hospital waiting on an update on Katrina's condition when they called for the family of Malik's son's mother, Kashari. When I heard the screams from her mother, I knew that she didn't make it, causing my tears to fall. I was afraid that we were going to meet the same fate as her family. Malik was flipping out, so Q had to grab him into a bear hug to stop him from trying to destroy the emergency room. My mother held on to me tight, rocking me in her arms, but my mind was elsewhere. I kind of blamed myself for what happened to Katrina. When she wanted to leave Q alone because she was afraid that something like this was going to happen, I talked her out of it. When she wanted no parts supporting him today, I convinced her to support him. So, it was my fault that she was even at the courthouse today. The guilt of it all was killing me inside and if she made it out of this, I swear I will never interfere with any decisions she makes when it comes to dealing with Q. I just prayed that God spared her because she didn't deserve to die like this. I swear I would switch places with her if I could. Aaron wanted to stay with me at the hospital, but once my mother and Katrina's mother arrived, I told him that it was best that he leaves. I didn't think anything was going to happen between him and Malik. I just didn't think that it was a good idea for him to be here right now. Katrina's aunt Laverne arrived to the hospital about thirty minutes later and she was now comforting Katrina's mom because she was a mess too.

They were finally calling for the family of Katrina and we all got up and walked to the room that the nurse escorted us to. It was probably the same room that they just had Kashari's family come in to tell them that she didn't make it. My body was shaking as I took a seat waiting for the surgeons to enter the room to give us an update on her condition. Q stood by the window with his head in his hands, probably praying that they didn't come in here telling us that she didn't make it. I tried to read the expression on the doctor's face, but I knew that he was probably trained to wear his game face. I had no idea what was going to come out of his mouth. I was nervously rambling in my head. To be honest, I was scared to hear anything that was about to come out of his mouth.

About an hour later, I sat in the hotel room in a confused dazed with the doctor voice telling us that my best friend was gone ringing in my ears. The guilt I was feeling was killing me inside even more now that she didn't make it. I don't know how I'm going to live with this pain that I was feeling right now knowing I was never going to see her again.

"Tamika baby, I need for you to eat something," my mother tried again.

Why didn't she understand that I could care less about eating ever again? Does she not understand that a piece of me was just taken from me? I didn't want to take it out on my mother, but I just need for her to leave me alone and just let me be. Aaron keeps calling me, so he wasn't getting the message just like she wasn't getting it. My friend is gone and I'm homeless. Just knowing that this nightmare I'm in is one that I will not be waking up from, is killing me inside. I know that I'm not the only one hurting right now but I just need time to try and process what's going on in my head right now. Q had to be placed in handcuffs at the hospital to detain him because he lost it when they told him that no one could see her just yet. I didn't feel sorry for him. Had he left her alone when she told him that she didn't feel safe, none of this would have happened like she predicted it would. It wasn't like he was being faithful being he was sleeping around on her every chance that he got. His ass was the blame too if you ask me. If he would have just left her alone, she would still be here.

Londyn

My mind took me back to the day she was so happy that he helped her up off the ground not caring that she could have been shot, causing me to laugh. I remember the time my mother lost her job when I was in middle school and she had to apply for government assistance. She sent me to the store to spend food stamps, but I was embarrassed, thinking that I was going to see friends from my school. I went to Katrina's house to get her to walk around the corner with me to the supermarket figuring she wouldn't be embarrassed, but she was. I stressed to her that I couldn't go back home without the groceries. So, she took a pack of ground beef and the garlic bread, stuck it in her jacket and walked out of the store. We laughed so hard that day as we ran all the way home, praying that my mother didn't ask for the receipt. Katrina always had my back and I'm going to miss that part of her the most. Who's going to be here for me now when I have my baby? I got up to go into the bathroom to take a shower after grabbing the bag of things my mom picked up for me. All we had right now was the clothes on our backs and the few things that she just picked up from Rainbow so that we could have something to put on to sleep in and wear tomorrow. I could tell that my mother was worried about what we were going to do now that we no longer have our apartment. I wished that she would have listened to me when I told her to sublease. It's not allowed to sublease a housing apartment but shit, I know people that do it all the time when they move out of state just in case it didn't work out.

When I got out of the shower, I saw the message indicator on my phone blinking. I grabbed my phone and it was a message from Aaron.

Aaron- I know that you don't feel like talking right now, but I just wanted to let you know that I'm here if you need me. Again, I'm sorry about Katrina. Call when you feel up to it.

I knew he meant well but I wasn't in the mood to talk to him or anyone else for that matter. All I wanted to do was close my eyes and shut down, even if it is only for one night.

When I woke up the next morning, my mother was sitting at the table with Katrina's mom, helping her make arrangements for Katrina's funeral. I heard her say that Q was going to pay for her funeral and whatever else that she needed, including somewhere to stay until she received the insurance money on the house, which included me and my mom also. Sounded like guilt money to me, but that's the least that he could do being I blamed him just as much as I blamed myself.

"How are you feeling this morning, baby?" My mother asked once she noticed that I was up.

Londyn

I just walked over to the table and hugged Katrina's mom not wanting to let go because she was the only thing of her that I had left.

"Tamika, I want you to be a part of the planning of her funeral because no one knew her the way that you knew her. I know that this is hard, but I promise you she would want you to tell me what she would want," she said to me.

She wasn't lying that Katrina would not have wanted her mother picking her outfit being she always stressed that her mother had no sense of style. That's why when she came to me to help with the outfits for Katrina for Christmas, I was all too happy to help her. I spent the rest of the morning helping her with the obituary and songs that would play at her service. When I tell you that it was the hardest thing that I ever had to do; it was the hardest. I was literally sick to my stomach and it had nothing to do with the baby that's growing inside of me. After Katrina's mom left, I finally called Aaron and he talked me into getting out of the hotel for a little while to take my mind off everything, so I agreed. He took me shopping' something that I didn't expect him to do because he never spent this much on me before. After shopping, he took me to get something to eat.

Giving My Heart to A Gangsta

We made small talk as we waited for them to bring us our food, but his line of questioning had me looking at him with the side eye. He was supposed to be here making me feel better about losing my best friend, but he was asking me about what happened with Q's court case, which I found strange. When he asked me did we receive the report about the fire from the investigator, I was taken back because it just happened yesterday. If they were doing an investigation how the hell would we have the report back. If he was the insurance company asking, maybe I would have given him the benefit of the doubt. But, it wasn't his business and he was turning me off. I didn't even want to eat, to be honest with you. I just wanted him to take me back to the hotel. I no longer wanted to be in his company and I have no idea if what I was now feeling towards him had anything to do with what Jemima told Katrina.

Chapter Twenty-Six
(Quentin)

Katrina being gone was now a reality after being at her funeral and seeing her lying in the soft pink casket looking to be sleeping peacefully. I should have listened to her when she wanted out being she knew in her heart that this would be her destiny if she continued a relationship with me. I wasn't treating her the way she deserved to be treated. Instead of trying to keep her with materialistic things, I should have proved my love by not cheating on her. A lot of shit wasn't sitting right with me and I wasn't going to dwell on the shit until my baby was laid to rest; so game on. It was true that I was creeping with Tierra, but we never had a conversation about her being pregnant by me. So, for them to say that she had text messages in her phone of her telling me that she was going to meet up with me to discuss the baby and how we were going to tell my girlfriend, it was a straight fucking lie. I don't know who the fuck was trying to set me up but being they arrested me on some charges that I assaulted Jemima, that's the bitch that I was going to start with. I have been following her ass all day, but nothing stood out to me until she left the nail salon after being picked up by Aaron. He had yet to pull away from the curb because they seemed to be arguing about something. I wanted to get out of the car to ask what the fuck was going on, but I decided to see how it played out. They sat in the car for about thirty minutes before she got out of the car and when she got out, she was carrying a backpack that she didn't have when she got in the car. Now my interest was really peaked. I watched her flag a cab and once she was in the cab, I followed closely behind until I saw that he was going into the direction of her apartment building. I slowed down because that yellow cab was going to have me getting pulled the fuck over trying to keep up with his driving recklessly ass.

Once I made it to her building, I stayed in my car and blazed a blunt before getting out to question this bitch. I knew that if she looked out the peephole and saw me, she wasn't going to answer the door, so I knocked on one of her neighbor's door and the bitch that answered the door looked like a straight feign. I offered the bitch a hundred dollars to knock on the door for me but not before telling that bitch if she mentions anything, I would come back and blow her fucking brains out. She looked scared, but she wasn't that damn scared. She took the money and stuffed it in her bra, making sure that I didn't snatch that shit back. I couldn't do shit but laugh as she switched her skinny ass down the hall to knock on Jemima's door with me standing to the side waiting for her to open that bitch. I guess the bitch didn't think that I was coming to see her ass because she opened the door without a care in the world. When I looked down, I saw the gun in her hand. Her neighbor ran so fast back to her apartment. For me, that gun didn't faze me as I walked up in her shit and locked the door behind me.

"Q, I didn't invite you in, so you need to leave," she stuttered as her hands shook.

"You need to put that gun down before your scary ass fuck around and shoot me," I told her, taking a seat on the couch.

She still stood there holding the gun and I was trying to be patient with her ass because I didn't like the idea of any fucking body pointing a gun at me. If she was going to shoot, her ass would have shot already, so she had one last chance to put it down before I bodied her ass.

"I'm giving you one last chance to put your gun away, Jemima, and get your ass over here so that we can talk," I told her.

She hesitantly put the gun down on the table. As soon as it was down, I walked over to her and slapped the shit out of her.

"Don't you ever pull a fucking gun out on me, bitch," I barked, pushing her down on the couch. "Do you know what happens to motherfuckers that call the law?" I asked her.

"Q, I didn't call anyone about you putting your hands on me. When Tierra was killed, I was questioned. When they told me that the two of you were messing around, I got pissed and mentioned that you hit me," she lied with a straight face.

"So, they questioned you, Jemima? Are you sure that you didn't tell them anything else because they questioned me about Tierra having a conversation with me about her being pregnant?"

"I, I didn't know that she was pregnant, Q. I'm still stuck on the fact that you were sleeping with my best friend," she tried letting a few tears fall.

I wasn't about to be up in here playing games with this grimy bitch because she knows just like I know that she's nothing but a fucking liar. If she didn't want to tell me the truth, I was going to force the shit out of her. If that meant killing the bitch and never knowing the truth, I was ok with that too. Nothing was going to bring Katrina back so killing this bitch and being done with it is where my head was at right now. I pulled out my gun from my waist to let this bitch know that I was serious and done playing with her ass.

"You better tell me the fucking truth, Jemima. Right now or I'm going to blow your fucking head off," I threatened.

"Tierra came to me as my friend to tell me the truth about the two of you a few months ago. She stressed how she was sorry and that it was never going to happen again. My stupid ass believed her. So much so that I didn't even question you about the fucking dog that you were to be sleeping with me and my best friend. When I found out that the two of you were still sleeping together, I approached her and that's when she told me that she was pregnant. I was hurt so I wanted you to hurt the same way that I was hurting. Being that I knew that you and Malik was responsible for killing Trey, I put my plan in motion. I knew that Raheem and Trey were cousins so I'm the one that told Raheem about you and Malik killing his cousin. Being he was doing business with you and Malik, he knew that it wouldn't be hard to avenge his death. It didn't quite pan out the way he wanted. Malik was still breathing and two of his niggas were dead. He knew that you were going to suspect foul play, so he fell back; but I still wanted you to pay. I might have fallen back too after Malik got shot being I felt bad, but you just kept being disrespectful and treating me like shit. The bitch who was my friend was still walking around carrying your baby after she said that she would get rid of it. I swear to you, I approached Aaron, telling him that I had some info on his girl, but I would only tell him if he did something for me. He was down but after I told him about Tamika messing around with Malik, he got in his feelings forgetting that he agreed to help me until I threatened that I would tell what I knew about him. He helped me get those charges pinned on you. I was the one that slit that bitch neck and set that fucking house on fire since you're buying houses for bitches. I killed that bitch for showing up to court after I told her about you and Tierra. I thought the bitch would have been smart enough to leave you the fuck alone so she's the reason she's no longer breathing," she finished.

"So, what's in the bag that Aaron gave you?" I asked her, still trying to process everything that she just told me.

My trigger finger was itching, but I wasn't ready to put this miserable bitch to sleep yet since I still had a few more questions. I needed to know how Aaron was able to get those charges with no fucking evidence because I know that I never had no fucking text messages in my phone about meeting up with Tierra.

"He gave me the gun and some money to get out of town until everything here died down," she admitted.

"Well, do you know that you took Malik's son's mother from him because of this jealous bullshit that you were on and still didn't get the fucking man?" I barked at her ass.

"She was at the wrong place at the wrong time," she spat, and I just looked at her because this wasn't the same gullible Jemima that I've been fucking.

It was easy to sit here and blame her for all that went down but I had to keep it real with myself knowing that it was my actions that caused this. They always say that a woman scorned was nothing to play with and this bitch here just proved that I fucked with the wrong bitch's heart. She fucked up too by giving her heart to a gangsta. At this point, I didn't give a fuck how Aaron was able to get those charges against me because the sight of her made me fucking sick to my stomach.

"Q, I'm pregnant," she blurted out once she saw me point the gun.

"Do you really think that I give a fuck about you being pregnant when you didn't care about Malik son not having a mother, Katrina being taken from her mother and Tierra who was carrying my seed? So, what reason do I have to spare you and your baby?" I asked this delusional bitch.

"Q, anything that I've ever done was for you so please, let's just start over and raise this baby together. Listen, if you spare my life, I'll tell you what I know about Aaron because he's the one that doesn't deserve to live," she rambled saying anything to keep me from pulling the trigger.

"What do you know about Aaron?" I asked her, letting her think that it was going to save her from taking this dirt nap.

"I met Aaron on the debate team, so we used to go and chill with him and a few others at his house at least once a week. The next week, it was just me, him and Katrina's brother, Troy chilling when Aaron started messing around with a gun from his father's closet. He accidently shot Troy that day and when I went to call 911 to get help, he convinced me that he would handle it. His uncle is a police detective and they handled it to make it look like a random shooting," she said, also letting me know where the bogus evidence came from.

This girl was a piece of fucking work and she really wanted me to spare her life, but she had another thing coming. I'm starting to see that you really can't judge a book by its cover. Aaron's ass was at the cabin smiling all up in Katrina's face knowing that he killed her brother. She thought he was just this nice person and felt bad for him when we fucked him up when his ass was nothing more than a fucking snake too.

"Wow, you are unbelievable to sit here and admit that you're a fucking murderer and an accessory to a murder and expect me to want to be with you. If you're pregnant, the best thing that you could do for that baby is to abort it. Especially if there is a chance he or she comes out to be just like you." I said, giving her hope that she was going to make it out here alive.

I already hit Malik up to let him know discreetly that I needed the Brady Bunch with her address in a text message while she was rambling on. I wasn't about to entertain her ass for another fucking minute; her time was up.

"When you get to hell, tell my uncle that I said hello," I told her before shooting her in the head twice, watching her lifeless body slump onto the floor.

Chapter Twenty-Seven
(Tamika)

"Are you sure that you're ok, Tamika? It seems like your mind is miles away," Aaron said to me.

We just left the restaurant and were now sitting in his car about to head to his place, but I was stalling for time.

"I'm ok, Aaron. It just feels like I have heartburn from those spicy meatballs. Do you think that you could stop at the Walmart so that I could get some chewable tums?" I asked him.

"Anything for you and my baby," he said, rubbing my stomach and making me cringe inside.

As soon as we pulled up to the Walmart parking lot, it wasn't too crowded; just as I thought it would be. This Walmart was never crowded this time of night. That's why I chose the restaurant close to this one.

"Are you coming inside, or do you want me to just pick it up for you?" He asked me, but I was distracted texting on my phone.

Londyn

"Wait; just give me a few minutes. I'm really feeling nauseous right now," I lied, holding my stomach and putting my head down moaning just a little.

"Do you want me to take you to the hospital?" He asked, concern written on his face.

"Let me just sit for a few more minutes to see if it stops. It might be because I just ate, and the motion of the car is what made me sick," I told him, trying to sound believable just as he was being pulled out of the car.

He should have known something was up when I didn't even scream, but he didn't. He was begging them not to hurt me, telling them that I was pregnant and to just let me go. They threw him into the trunk and Malik came and helped me out of the car, putting me in his car. Q and some dude that I didn't know, pulled off in the beat-up Honda that held Aaron inside and we pulled out after them.

"Are you ok?" Malik asked me, but I was a little ticked off because getting in the car with him wasn't part of the plan.

The last time I saw him was at the hospital when they told him that his son's mother didn't make it, so I decided to be cordial.

Giving My Heart to A Gangsta

"I'm ok and I didn't get the chance to tell you that I was sorry about what happened to your son's mother," I offered.

"Thank you. That shit fucked me up because her nor Katrina deserved to go out like that," he responded sadly.

"I'm still having a tough time believing that she's gone being I have to keep catching myself from dialing her number. Not a day goes by that I don't blame myself for her not being here. I was the one that talked her into going to the courthouse," I admitted, causing a few tears to fall.

"This is not your fault, Tamika. Whether it was the courthouse or her coming out of her house, that bitch Jemima was gunning for her. She wasn't going to let Q and Katrina be together, so she wouldn't have stopped until she succeeded with getting her out the picture."

"I know but it's just hard not to blame myself when she was set on leaving him alone, Had I not intervened, she probably would still be alive."

"She may have left him alone, but trust me, he wasn't going to leave her alone. That would have set Jemima's crazy ass off too. The only person to blame for Katrina being gone is Jemima and her ass will never hurt anyone else because she was sent straight to hell."

263

Londyn

It really didn't make me feel any better that they handled Jemima because it wasn't going to bring my friend back. I'm not saying I regret the day that I invited them to my house, but I do regret not getting out when Katrina wanted us too. I think that when I finish school, my mom and I will be leaving New York. There are too many bad memories here. I just want to start over and raise my baby in a safe environment where I don't have to worry about getting gunned down by someone behind all the bad blood in these streets. If these niggas think that I'm carrying Malik's baby, I'm always going to be a target being he's going to always be in the streets.

I know that they believe gunning Aaron down is the right thing, but it's not going to bring Katrina's brother back. I honestly believe that it's going to start a hit for a hit and I want no parts of any of it. I'm done with this 'loving a gangsta' lifestyle.

"Can you take me back to the hotel?" I asked him.

I thought that I wanted to be there to see them put a bullet in Aaron's head, but I changed my mind because I still had love for him. This could very well be his baby that I'm carrying so I probably would beg them not to kill him. I rather not be there.

"No problem," was all he said as he headed in the direction of the hotel.

I think he was in his feelings knowing that I still cared for Aaron being I didn't want to watch him be killed. I would have felt the same way if it was him about to take a bullet to the head because I still cared for him too. I just was ready to put it all behind me for the sake of my unborn child that I have fallen in love with.

"So, are you still going to give me a DNA test once the baby is born?" He asked, causing me to sigh.

I know that he has a right to know if this is his baby that I'm carrying, but I just wanted to raise my baby on my own. I know that he's not going to understand it if I tell him that, so I was just going to say what I needed to say to appease him for now. I may have a change of heart how I feel but right now I'm going to stick to getting the hell out of New York with my mother and raise my child without a father.

"Malik, I don't have a problem giving you a DNA test once the baby is born," I lied.

"Tamika, I just want to apologize for all the pain that I caused you and if you never believed anything that I ever said to you, believe that I loved you."

Londyn

If how he did me was him loving me, I promise you that I never want to be in love again because love isn't supposed to hurt.

"I loved you too Malik and I apologize for lying to you," I told him.

I regret playing with them both because in the end, no one wins and now a baby will be born not knowing who the hell her father is. When we pulled up to the hotel, I wiped the tears that fell from my eyes before looking at Malik, telling him thank you, knowing that he probably wouldn't be seeing me again.

"No problem. If you need anything, and I do mean anything, give me a call," he said, reaching over and kissing me on the lips.

Damn, I thought. He never kissed me like this before, so I honestly believed that he knew this was goodbye for us. He slipped his tongue into my mouth and I returned the kiss, getting caught up in the moment; I still cared for him. He started to caress my breast, causing me to moan, wanting to feel him inside of me as I allowed him to undress me like we weren't in a fucking car. My head was resting against the window as his head rested between my legs feasting on my pussy. The position that we were in was uncomfortable but with the feeling that he was giving me, I didn't mind the cramp that I was going to feel from my neck being pushed up against the window. He must have been uncomfortable too because he told me to climb into the backseat where he fucked the shit out of me. I didn't know what the hell was wrong with me. I just convinced myself that once I got out of the car I would never see him again, to letting him have my pregnant ass fucking in the back of his car. I can admit that I got caught up in the moment. I gathered my clothes, telling him thanks again for the ride, before taking my ass inside of the hotel.

After getting out of the shower, I went into the living area of the hotel where my mother was sitting with the newspaper in her hand. I was praying that she didn't lose her job because we were already in a bad financial situation.

"Are you looking for a job?" I asked her, again praying that she wasn't.

"No, I'm looking for an apartment, but everything is so expensive. Living here in this damn hotel is expensive too. I was hoping to find something affordable but with no such luck," she responded.

Londyn

"I thought that we were going to move out of state after I graduate. I'm not trying to raise my baby in New York," I said to her.

I wasn't trying to stay in New York and I have no idea why she was changing what we already talked about and agreed to. If she thinks that I'm staying here, she had another thing coming because I already made up my mind that we were leaving in a few months.

"Well, if you're not trying to raise a baby in New York then you shouldn't have gotten pregnant," she snapped.

"Mom, I wasn't trying to get pregnant; it just happened," my voice cracked, not believing that she just said that to me.

"What did you expect to happen when you're running around here sleeping with two men unprotected? I knew that I shouldn't have listened to you when I allowed you to talk me into taking a handout from your hood boyfriend. We went from having to paying nothing to paying the price of being homeless," she ranted.

I understood that she was frustrated but taking it out on me was wrong. I never forced her hand to take what she is now calling a hand-out. Her words hit me like a ton of bricks as I allowed the tears to fall from my eyes. She was the parent and she could have easily said no, but she didn't. She was never that parent that gave a fuck about what her child was doing and who she was doing it with. So, to belittle me for getting pregnant hurt me. She needed to take some responsibility and think that maybe she failed me as a parent since her daughter was sleeping with two men. Doesn't that mean that she wasn't paying attention, or she didn't care to know what I was doing when she wasn't at home? I would never say that to her. At the end of the day, she was my mother. I would never disrespect my mother and the fact that I love her. I know that she loves me too. The stress of our situation is bringing out her true feelings about my being pregnant. Shit, I'm stressed too.

I just wished that Katrina was still alive because having her made life so much easier for times like these when I just wanted to end it all. I needed her more than I needed air right now. I knew she was never coming back so I was on my own to figure it out. My tears continued to fall and all I wanted was my mother to pull me into her arms and tell me that everything was going to be alright. She got up and I thought she was going to do just that, but she grabbed her bag and walked out of the hotel room, letting the door slam behind her. She really had me second guessing my decision about not letting Malik be a part of this baby's life even if it was just for financial means. I knew that this baby was going to be a burden on her and I didn't want that. If she was going to stay in New York, I knew that I probably was going to end up on assistance from the government. The thought of it all made my tears fall harder as I got up from the table going into the bathroom. I sat in the bathroom for a few minutes trying to gather my thoughts before washing my face and heading out of the bathroom. I heard my phone ringing at the same time someone was knocking at the door. I looked to see that it was Malik calling but I didn't answer because I couldn't leave my mother standing at the door.

When I opened the door and saw Aaron standing there with blood soak clothes and a gun pointed in my face, my heart stopped momentarily. My life flashed before my eyes as my mind took me back to when Katrina and I were sitting on her bedroom floor playing with dolls. We were talking about who we were going to marry but we weren't like the other little girls who dreamed of marrying a doctor or a lawyer. We always said that we were going to marry a big-time drug dealer who had lots of money and cars. If I knew what I know now, I would have been just like the other little girls. As I stood at this door, I regretted the day that I decided that I wanted to play a game that I had no idea that I wasn't going to win. Life has a funny way of allowing you to see things clear as day when it's too late to do anything about it. I now see all the hurt and pain that I caused Aaron by looking into his eyes as he pointed that gun at me. What I didn't see was sympathy. I didn't see any sympathy for me or the child I was carrying, leaving me regretting my decision to giving my heart to a gangsta before he pulled the trigger and stood over me until I took my last breath.

CPSIA information can be obtained
at www.ICGtesting.com
Printed in the USA
LVHW08s0912290918
591585LV00022B/547/P

9 781986 878944